"I'll make a deal with you."

"What kind of deal?" It was painfully obvious that he made Hadley nervous.

"I'm going to be stuck in this town for a while. You introduce me around, and if your unwanted suitor gets the wrong idea, we'll both be happy."

"I suppose we *could* go to the Tipped Barrel. I've never been there—or any other bar. When people see me there, they'll be certain you're corrupting me." She smiled suddenly. Brilliantly. "Okay. Let's go."

"You don't want to change clothes or anything?"

Her enthusiasm visibly faltered and Dane felt like kicking himself. He caught her chin in his fingers and lifted. "You don't *need* to change," he said gruffly. "You're perfect the way you are."

She didn't look convinced. And standing there touching her face—satin smooth and velvet soft and, if he wasn't mistaken, completely devoid of artifice—wasn't the smartest thing he'd ever done in his life. Because he definitely wasn't soft. At all.

Dear Reader,

It's hard to believe that it's *that* time of year again—and what better way to escape the holiday hysteria than with a good book…or six! Our selections begin with Allison Leigh's *The Truth About the Tycoon,* as a man bent on revenge finds his plans have hit a snag—in the form of the beautiful sister of the man he's out to get.

THE PARKS EMPIRE concludes its six-book run with *The Homecoming* by Gina Wilkins, in which Walter Parks's daughter tries to free her mother from the clutches of her unscrupulous father. Too bad the handsome detective working for her dad is hot on her trail! *The M.D.'s Surprise Family* by Marie Ferrarella is another in her popular miniseries THE BACHELORS OF BLAIR MEMORIAL. This time, a lonely woman looking for a doctor to save her little brother finds both a healer of bodies and of hearts in the handsome neurosurgeon who comes highly recommended. In *A Kiss in the Moonlight,* another in Laurie Paige's SEVEN DEVILS miniseries, a woman can't resist her attraction to the man she let get away—because guilt was pulling her in another direction. But now he's back in her sights—soon to be in her clutches? In Karen Rose Smith's *Which Child Is Mine?* a woman is torn between the child she gave birth to and the one she's been raising. And the only way out seems to be to marry the man who fathered her "daughter." Last, a man decides to reclaim everything he's always wanted, in the form of his biological daughters, and their mother, in Sharon De Vita's *Rightfully His.*

Here's hoping every one of your holiday wishes comes true, and we look forward to celebrating the New Year with you.

All the best,

Gail Chasan
Senior Editor

Please address questions and book requests to:
Silhouette Reader Service
U.S.: 3010 Walden Ave., P.O. Box 1325, Buffalo, NY 14269
Canadian: P.O. Box 609, Fort Erie, Ont. L2A 5X3

The Truth About
the Tycoon

ALLISON LEIGH

SPECIAL EDITION®

Published by Silhouette Books

America's Publisher of Contemporary Romance

For my friends, old and new.

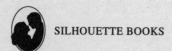 SILHOUETTE BOOKS

ISBN 0-373-24651-X

THE TRUTH ABOUT THE TYCOON

Copyright © 2004 by Allison Lee Davidson

This edition published by arrangement with Harlequin Books S.A.

® and TM are trademarks of Harlequin Books S.A., used under license.
Trademarks indicated with ® are registered in the United States Patent
and Trademark Office, the Canadian Trade Marks Office and in other
countries.

Visit Silhouette Books at www.eHarlequin.com

Printed in U.S.A.

Books by Allison Leigh

Silhouette Special Edition

Stay... #1170
The Rancher and the Redhead #1212
A Wedding for Maggie #1241
A Child for Christmas #1290
Millionaire's Instant Baby #1312
Married to a Stranger #1336
Mother in a Moment #1367
Her Unforgettable Fiancé #1381
The Princess and the Duke #1465
Montana Lawman #1497
Hard Choices #1561
Secretly Married #1591
Home on the Ranch #1633
The Truth About the Tycoon #1651

*Men of the Double-C Ranch

ALLISON LEIGH

started early by writing a Halloween play that her grade-school class performed. Since then, though her tastes have changed, her love for reading has not. And her writing appetite simply grows more voracious by the day.

She has been a finalist in the RITA® Award and the Holt Medallion contests. But the true highlights of her day as a writer are when she receives word from a reader that they laughed, cried or lost a night of sleep while reading one of her books.

Born in Southern California, Allison has lived in several different cities in four different states. She has been, at one time or another, a cosmetologist, a computer programmer and a secretary. She has recently begun writing full-time after spending nearly a decade as an administrative assistant for a busy neighborhood church, and currently makes her home in Arizona with her family. She loves to hear from her readers, who can write to her at P.O. Box 40772, Mesa, AZ 85274-0772.

Dear Reader,

What can I say about Dane Rutherford? He's hovered in my mind since his sister, Darby, found love with Garrett Cullum in *Mother in a Moment*. So, I was particularly pleased when his story finally "perked" its way to the surface. I thoroughly enjoyed spending time with Dane and Hadley, and then when Nikki Day briefly found her way to Hadley's boardinghouse, Tiff's, there was a wonderful sense of connection for me. The Rutherford clan was now connected to some of my favorite folks from Weaver, Wyoming, and the entire Double-C Ranch family. I felt like my old friends had come to have a party together! Of course, Nikki's fate—also hinted at in her twin's story in *Home on the Ranch*—still needs to be determined, so I hope you'll all stay tuned! In the meantime, thank you for sharing some time with Dane and Hadley. I hope you enjoy the party as much as I did.

My very best wishes,

Allison

Chapter One

The pickup truck pulled out right in front of him.

Dane Rutherford swore a blue streak, wrenching his steering wheel. He missed clipping the hind end of the pickup by the breadth of a fat snowflake and shot past, close enough to see the panic widening a pair of already wide female eyes as the driver of the pickup turned to see his car.

He was still swearing as he fishtailed on the slick road, turning into the skid, trying to regain control. And though he'd missed the pickup at first, the skid caused metal to meet metal in a long, eerie scrape. They still would have been okay if she hadn't panicked at the contact. But she did. And she careened one way, then the other.

Dane cursed anew, trying to avoid hitting her again.

The road was winding, as damnably narrow as any back road he'd ever raced, and he felt his stomach drop out as his car went airborne off the shoulder, over the ditch.

Then he forgot about whether the woman was okay, about what Wood would say when he learned Dane had smashed his precious car, about everything except bracing himself for the impact.

The car was old. The tree it hit was older. Solid as hell, and there was no way Dane could hope to avoid it.

Crashing into it should at least stop the car's flight.

It did. Effectively.

Hadley stared in disbelief at the way the front end of the cherry-red car accordioned against the massive poplar tree trunk. She was so focused on the other vehicle, in fact, that she very nearly forgot her own problems. Gasping, she jerked the steering wheel again to keep from going down the opposite ditch and then cringed when she plowed right into the mileage marker on the side of the road, hard enough to bend the thing clean over.

She sat there for a moment. Stunned.

The engine gasped. Groaned. The sad sounds were enough to break her momentary shock, and she quickly turned off the engine before it surely died.

More work for Stu to do on her vehicle.

Shaking her head to clear it, she looked back for the other car. The roadside ditch it had plunged down was deep and she couldn't even see the car.

"*Please* be okay," she muttered under her breath as she pushed out into the snowy afternoon, racing across the road. Her boots skidded as she dashed down the opposite shoulder, and her feet flew out from beneath her. Her hands flailed, her rear hitting the unrelentingly frozen earth of the steep incline. She barely felt the jarring impact shoot up her body to her teeth, which slammed together, before she was pushing to her feet again, slipping and sliding her way to the crumpled car. She couldn't get to the driver's side.

"Please be okay." Her voice was a prayer this time as she rounded the hiked-up rear of the vehicle. One of the back wheels was still slowly spinning. She leaned down, peering through the spidery web of the cracked side window.

The man's head was thrown back against the headrest. Blood splattered the inside of the windshield where he'd obviously hit his head, and it freely flowed from his forehead. The car hadn't possessed an air bag, either.

The sight of all that blood sent alarm careening through her. "Hey." She frantically tried to open the wrinkled door but it wouldn't budge. Knocking on the cracked window was out of the question. And the engine was still running. She reached out and thumped her hand on the crumpled hood of the car, since pounding on the white convertible top wasn't going to do any good in gaining his attention, but his eyes remained closed, unmoving. "Lord," she whispered fearfully, "please let him be okay." She banged on the car again. Hard enough to make her hand ache. Peered through the window. "Yessss." His chest had moved. *Was* moving.

Thank you, God.

He was alive.

She scrambled out of the ditch and ran across the road, nearly tripping over her feet. Her fingers were so cold she could barely open her truck door. But she managed, and she leaned across the bench seat, grabbing her purse that had fallen on the floor. She dumped it out on the seat and snatched up her cell phone. It took two tries to punch the number. She clutched it to her ear as she dashed back across the road. Slid down on her rear again to get to the car. A thin dusting of snow now covered the crumpled hood.

"Shane, answer your darned phone." She ran around to the side of the car again, banging her numb palm against the door. "Hey. Come on, mister, wake up. Oh, Shane." She hunched over, holding the phone tightly when she heard her brother's voice. "Thank heavens. There's an accident—no, I'm fine."

The man inside the car stirred. "Oh. Hey." She waved her arms. As if he'd notice through his eyelids. "Unlock the car door." She banged again on the hood. Even kicked at the side a little.

His head raised up. Impossibly thick lashes lifted to reveal a slit of dark eyes.

"That's it, that's it." She patted the car as if she were patting a good dog. "Come on. Wake up."

She realized her brother was yelling her name through the cell phone. "Sorry, Shane. We're about a quarter mile past Stu's turnoff. Better send the ambulance." She pressed the off button on her brother's tight voice and stuffed the phone into her pocket, where it immediately began vibrating again. She ignored it in favor of the man inside the vehicle. He'd touched his forehead. Was staring at the blood his fingers came away with.

"Unlock the door," she said loudly again.

He eyed her. Sat forward a little, only to grimace. She read his lips easily enough. Swearing. She chose to take that as a good sign. His arm slowly moved and she heard a soft snick. He'd unlocked the door. She yanked hard on it to get it to budge and wedged her leg inside when it did. The stressed window crumbled into fine dust and a rush of warm air came out at her as she worked herself in, reaching straight across for the ignition.

She turned the key.

The laboring engine fell silent.

Her heart was pounding so hard she thought for certain he could hear it. She looked at him and realized that she was practically in his face. His…very attractive face, what there was she could see beneath the bloody smears. She hurriedly shifted, putting space between them, kneeling awkwardly on the seat beside him. The stubborn door was practically crushing her leg and she shoved hard on it with her snow boot to keep it open.

"Who the hell taught you how to drive?" His voice was deep, even if it was little more than a murmur.

She tried not to cringe. "My father, Beau Golightly."

The man shifted, groaned a little, and she gently pressed her hands against his shoulder. "You shouldn't move. There's an ambulance on the way." She dragged her sweater sleeve down over her hand from beneath the edge of her coat and gingerly pressed it against his temple, blotting some of the blood.

He closed a surprisingly strong hand over hers, staying the movements. "I don't need a bloody ambulance."

"Well, *you* are bloody," she returned, carefully sliding her hand from beneath his. "Literally." Even as she voiced the observation, she heard a siren whine. "My brother Shane is probably burning rubber to get here, too. He's the sheriff."

For a moment the driver looked irritated. But he said nothing. Merely unclipped his seat belt and peered out the windshield at the mangled hood of his car. "You're joking about the Golightly thing, aren't you?" he finally asked.

She frowned a little. "No. And I know how to drive just fine." Defense came belatedly, but at least it came. "You were the one playing Speed Racer."

His lips twisted a little. "Not anymore," she thought she heard him mutter. But it was hard to tell since the ambulance's siren was earsplitting in the moments before it wheezed to a halt. She finished backing out of the car and looked over to see Palmer Frame, and his latest sidekick, Noah Hanlan, slip-sliding down into the ditch. The ambulance waited on the shoulder up above them.

Palmer's gaze traveled over her. "You hurt, Hadley?"

She shook her head and waved her hand toward the driver where Noah was making his way. "He is. He's—"

"Fine."

"—bleeding. A lot." She ignored the clipped comment from inside the wreck and moved out of Palmer's way. The tan SUV her brother drove screamed up the highway, and she sighed a little as she climbed up the embankment once more. It took some doing, since she kept looking back over her shoulder to see how Palmer and Noah were progressing with the injured man.

The EMTs had produced a crowbar and had worked the door open wide enough for the driver to get out. Standing, he was just as tall or taller than Palmer, and that was saying something. But he *was* standing, which meant he couldn't be too bad off, right?

She hoped.

A part of her heard the crunch of tires, a fast stop. Shane's tight voice muttering her name more like a curse than a prayer.

The driver had shaken off Palmer's assistance, she noted. He'd planted his feet in the snow, hands on hips as he surveyed his car.

Very fine hips. Verrry fine rear—

"Hadley!"

She closed her eyes, whispered another quick prayer for patience—her tenth that day, at least—and stuck out her hand toward her brother. The ditch was getting more slippery by the minute and the late-afternoon temperature seemed to be dropping by chunks. "Help me up."

Shane's voice might have been annoyed, but his eyes were sharp with concern as he pulled her up the rest of the way to the road. His hands clamped on her shoulders as he examined her face.

Relief filled his eyes though his stern expression didn't relax much. Evidently satisfied that Hadley was unharmed, he let go of her and headed into the ditch, pulling out the small notepad he carried in one of the pockets of his shearling coat. The sheriff, back at work.

Hadley shivered, wishing her own wool jacket were as warm as her brother's. But she'd bought her jacket because of its pretty pink color, not because of its ability to keep the cold at bay. It was one of her ridiculously few frivolous purchases.

The three men were now staring at the car, looking as if they were in mourning or something. Well, the car did look pretty sad. It was old to start with, though the paint job—on the rear of the car at least— looked in perfect shape. She, however, was more concerned about the driver and his injuries than the front bumper that was now kissing cousins to the windshield wipers. For heaven's sake, it was just a car. And the man was *still* bleeding. She could tell, because he'd swiped a hand over his forehead, and more blood oozed out to replace what he wiped away.

She stomped her way back into the ditch, tugging at Palmer and Noah. The men were EMTs, not car mechanics. ''Don't you think you ought to be seeing to *him?*'' She looked up at the injured driver.

Snowflakes were catching in his thick hair. And he had ridiculously long black lashes, she noticed again, when he turned his gaze toward her. Steely blue. Until then, she'd never really known what that term defined, even though she'd used it herself when she was writing.

Now she knew firsthand. And…well. *Hello.*

She swallowed and took a step back, only to have her boot sink about a foot into the snow. Off balance, she felt herself falling, but the man shot out a hand and grabbed her upper arm to catch her. "You don't know much about being careful, do you?" he observed.

Instead of falling ignominiously back on her tush, she'd ended up leaning against him. And what a *him* he was. Her vivid imagination immediately tripped along the path of whether or not his body was as solid as it seemed beneath the leather bomber jacket he wore.

She planted her feet more securely, pushing herself upright. Men like him did not look at women like her, particularly when said woman had helped send his car crashing into a tree.

"*I* wasn't speeding," she pointed out, yet again. But her conscience bit at that. She didn't know if the man had been speeding or not. She'd been too preoccupied with her darned fool brothers and their unwelcome interest in her nonexistent love life.

Shane, Palmer and Noah were still dolefully shaking their heads over the crumpled car. "Um…maybe it's escaped everyone's notice, but you *are* still bleeding there." She waved her hand generally in his direction. Then happened to notice the fingerprints he'd left on her coat. Bloody fingerprints.

He noticed, as well, and grimaced a little. "Sorry about that."

She exhaled, impatient with the lot of them, and turned away. Climbed up the side of the ditch again and strode to the back of the ambulance where she yanked open the rear door. She grabbed a container of wipes and cleaned the blood from her hands, then grabbed a handful of gauze pads and headed back down the ditch.

Lordy, but her legs were starting to ache with all this up and downing. She tore open the paper wrapping on one of the pads and reached up, gingerly dabbing the injured man's forehead.

He jerked a little, grabbed her hand. "What are you doing?"

"Trying to help you," she reminded. But if the man didn't want assistance, fine. *She* didn't stick her nose in where it wasn't wanted. Unlike some specific siblings she could name. She pushed the pads into his hands and gave Palmer a stern poke in the ribs. "I've got things to do."

"Hold on there." Shane closed his hand over her collar, stopping her cold. "There's a small matter of the accident report."

Of course. Stupid of her. She could feel her face flushing and hoped that the man hadn't noticed. A lightning-quick glance his way quickly killed that little hope. "Fine. Could we do it out of the snow, though? Maybe *you* haven't noticed, but it is a little cold out here." Her words were visible puffs, ringing around her head. Since New Year's the week before, the weather had plummeted, bringing with it an uncommon amount of snow.

She was relieved when Shane looked again at the wreckage, then nodded. The driver apparently didn't find the EMTs' assistance objectionable the way he had hers. But then, they hadn't helped his car fly into a ditch, either.

Shane told her to go wait in his SUV, and she was shaken enough that she obediently turned away and started up the incline again. She heard her brother ask the driver if the registration for the vehicle was in the car as she went. Shane's SUV was idling, and she climbed up into the passenger seat where it was toasty warm. She flexed her numb fingers in front of the air vents and watched the men.

Of course there would have to be an accident report. No need to worry over it. The worst that would happen is that her insurance rates would go up.

Again.

She rubbed her hands together. Cupped her fingers over her mouth and nose and blew on them. She loved living in Lucius, Montana, but honestly, there were times she'd be happy to spend the winter lolling on a warm, sandy beach somewhere. If she closed her eyes, she could practically feel the heated kiss of sunlight on her face.

"Hand me that clipboard."

The only warmth came from Shane's heater vents. She opened her eyes to see her brother standing inside the opened door, his gloved finger pointing at the items on his console.

She handed the clipboard to him. Looked around his broad shoulder to see that the driver was now sitting on the back of the ambulance, submitting to Palmer's belated but thorough examination. She could see Noah behind the wheel talking on the mic. "Hate that paperwork," she murmured lightly, eyeing her brother.

He grunted. "Be glad neither one of you was hurt. Otherwise there'd be a helluva lot more."

"I am." She couldn't have lived with herself if she'd harmed someone else. Still, she'd never been fond of putting her name on a bunch of legal documents. A trait passed down from her mother. "Shane—"

"Don't sweat it, turnip," he advised after a moment.

She rolled her eyes at the old nickname, but subsided against the seat. The interior was getting cold. She had on a wool jacket and Shane's heater was blasting. The driver wore only a leather bomber jacket. He'd surely be freezing by now. "Couldn't Palmer give him a blanket or something?"

Shane glanced over his shoulder. "S'pose so," he agreed, then turned his attention back to the report he was writing, his gaze sliding over her. "Stu was yakking my ear off on the phone about the way you ran out on him and Wendell when *you* called."

"What'd he think you were going to do? Arrest me because I didn't stick around until he could force me into having dinner with Wendell Pierce as well as lunch? Give me a break." Stu had manipulated her into going out to his ranch, playing on her sympathies to cook a meal for him since his left hand was currently in a cast, knowing full well that she'd be too polite to walk back out again when she found Wendell there, too.

She peered around Shane again. The driver was watching her and she felt the impact of his striking gaze across the yards. Her skin prickled.

It was a decidedly unusual sensation.

"Stu wants you to be happy and settled."

"Like the two of you are?" She forced herself to

look back at her brother, raising her eyebrows point-edly. "Like Evie is?" She shook her head. Neither of her brothers were married, or currently involved with anyone for that matter. And their sister, Evie, was…well, Evie was another story entirely. "It's pretty humiliating that my own brothers think I can't find a man for myself," she said half under her breath.

Even if it were true.

Not that she intended to admit it. She was already a pathetic marshmallow where her family was con-cerned. No need to provide them with her more am-munition.

"You're twenty-seven," Shane said. "When's the last time you went on a date?" His pen scratched across the paper. "With someone *other* than Wendell Pierce."

One lunch inadvertently shared at the counter of the Luscious Lucius did not really qualify as a date in her opinion, and she hadn't ever intended to repeat it, not even in the sunny kitchen of Stu's ranch house. But if she didn't count that…well then, she really *was* pathetic.

There was nothing *wrong* with Wendell, except that she had little in common with the brown-haired, tall, gangly forty-year-old rancher and even less of an attraction for him.

"Maybe I've been busy. Watching Evie's kids. Helping Stu out at the garage whenever Riva's gone. Doing *your* filing down at the station." All when she wasn't busy with her own responsibilities at Tiff's, the family's boardinghouse, and trying to carve out enough time on her own to do what she loved best—writing.

Shane barely gave her a second glance. He finished scratching on his clipboard, and strode across the highway toward her pickup truck, studying the snowy blacktop as he went. A wrecker had pulled up on the shoulder, and Hadley saw Gordon and Freddie Finn get out and slide their way down the embankment.

She closed the door again to preserve the heat and nibbled the inside of her lip as she watched Gordon hook up the wreckage to chains and slowly maneuver it back up the incline. It didn't seem possible, but the car looked even worse as it peeled away from the tree trunk.

She looked over at the driver again. His expression was unreadable, but a muscle flexed rhythmically in his jaw. She recognized that type of movement, having seen it often enough over the years on Shane's face.

She sighed a little, hauled in a deep breath and pushed open the truck door. She walked over to him and was grateful when he didn't just sort of duck and run for cover. He undoubtedly considered her a menace. ''I'm sorry about your car,'' she offered. It came out more tentative than she'd have liked, but then, so much about her did. What was one more instance to add to a lifetime of them? ''Have you had it a long time?''

''Long enough.'' His voice was surprisingly neutral, given the circumstances.

''Indiana,'' she murmured, spying the license plate on his car. ''Where were you heading?''

"Why?" His gaze sliced her way.

She lifted her shoulders, hugging her arms to herself. "Most people come through Lucius on their way to somewhere else. We're barely a bump in the road." Maybe that was a slight understatement. Lucius had its own hospital, its own schools and three different churches. There was also a fairly decent crop of restaurants and even a movie theater, complete with four screens. "I, um, have a cell phone if you need to call anyone." He didn't wear a wedding ring, but that didn't have to mean anything.

And why she was noticing his ring finger she had no idea. Hadn't she spent ten minutes that day already railing at Stu that she was *not* looking for a husband?

His lips twisted a little. She thought he almost looked amused. Almost. "No, thanks."

Which didn't exactly say that he'd had no one to call.

She shifted. Pushed her fingers into the pockets of her jacket. Freddie had climbed up on the back of the tow truck and was guiding the chains in some complicated fashion as her brother controlled a lever. The car creaked and moaned as it was pulled upward onto the slanted ramp. She winced a little and looked up at the man again. "Does your head hurt very badly?"

"Not as much as the car hurts." As if he couldn't stand to look at it any longer, he turned his attention to her pickup, where a good portion of candy-apple red from his car was decorating the side of her truck. It was the brightest color on what was otherwise pretty indeterminate.

"Is Palmer going to take you in to the hospital?"

"No."

She was surprised. "Palmer's a great EMT. The best. So's Noah. But you should probably still see a doctor about your head."

"It's not that bad."

"Are you sure? I thought head injuries were tricky. What if you have a concussion or something?"

"Then I'll deal with it."

He didn't sound as if he were used to being questioned, and she bit back more comments.

Shane had clearly finished looking at whatever he'd figured needing looking at and was heading toward them again. He held out his clipboard to the driver. "Fill that out. I'll need to see your license, too."

The man didn't take the clipboard. "We can settle this matter without all that." His voice brooked no disagreement, and Hadley mentally sat back a little, curious to see how her brother, I-am-sheriff-hear-me-roar, reacted.

"Some reason you don't want to file an accident report?" Shane's voice had turned that silky way it did whenever he was really displeased. He knew where Hadley's distaste for accident reports came from, she knew. But a stranger wouldn't be accorded a similar understanding.

Nevertheless, the driver looked unfazed, despite the gauze and tape covering half of his forehead. "Just the time it all takes," he said. "Neither one of us is hurt and we both agree to pay for our own damages."

Hadley made an involuntary sound, looking pointedly at his forehead. The truth was, they hadn't agreed to anything.

"My sister pulls out in front of you, and you're willing to cover the damages on your own car." Shane's gaze shifted to the vehicle in question that was now secured atop the flatbed of the tow truck. "That's a '68 Shelby."

The driver's expression didn't change. "I was going too fast. We're both culpable."

Shane sighed a little. Settled his snow-dusted cowboy hat on his head a little more squarely. "I can measure the skid marks," he said, all conversational-like. "To prove the point. But we both know what I'm gonna find." His smile was cool. "You weren't speeding. So that just leaves me a mite curious as to why you're in a such a hurry to go no place."

"I have business to attend to." The driver *still* seemed unfazed, and Hadley had to admire him for it. Not many people could stand their ground against that particular smile of Shane Golightly's. Even Stu, Shane's twin, had been known to back down in the face of it.

If the man wanted to claim a share of responsibility in the accident, who was she to argue? After all, she didn't particularly want that report filed, either.

Shane appeared to be considering the driver's smooth explanation. "Well. The registration is in order." He tapped a folded piece of paper that was still in his possession. "Let's just look at your license for now. Then we'll see."

The driver's expression didn't change one whit. "I don't have it on me."

Oh, dear. Hadley looked down at her boots, scuffling them a little in the skiff of snow.

"Well, that's kind of a problem now, isn't it?" Shane's voice was pleasant.

She closed her eyes. Shane never sounded that pleasant unless he was completely and totally peeved.

The driver didn't *look* like a car thief. Not that she necessarily knew what car thieves looked like. But if she were going to write one into one of her stories, she wouldn't have given him thick, chestnut-colored hair and vivid blue eyes with a rear end that was world class. She'd have given him piercings and tattoos and slick grease in his hair, and he *definitely* wouldn't be the hero—

She jerked her thoughts back to front and center. "Shane," she said in that dreaded, tentative voice of hers. "You don't have to give him the third-degree, surely. Mister, um—" she glanced up at the driver and simply lost her train of thought when his gaze found hers and held.

"Wood," he said.

Dear Lord, please don't let him be a car thief. He's just too pretty for that. "Pardon me?"

"Wood," he said again. "Tolliver. Atwood, actually, but nobody calls me that." The corner of his lips twisted. "Not if they want me to answer."

There was a molasses quality in his deep voice, she realized. Faint, but definitely Southern. And it was about as fine to listen to as her dad's singing every Sunday morning. When she was alive, her mother's voice had possessed a similar drawl.

With a start she realized she was staring at him.

Again. It was even more of a start to find that he was staring at her right back. Her skin prickled again, and it was not at all unpleasant.

"Well, *At*wood Tolliver," Shane said, still in that dangerously pleasant way. "I'm afraid I'm going to have to bring you in. Just till we verify that you really are who you say you are."

The driver's eyes froze over a little, and the hot little prickles underneath the surface of her skin turned as cold as the air seeping through her too-thin jacket.

Of course the man was staring at her. Undoubtedly wishing he'd never had the misfortune to drive anywhere near Lucius, Montana, *or* her.

The best-looking guy she'd ever seen in her entire life—on television, the movies or in her imagination—and her brother was gearing up to arrest him.

Chapter Two

Bring him in?

It wasn't often that Dane didn't get what he wanted. But right now, he'd hit the trifecta in that regard. Judging by the sheriff's implacable expression, Dane was not going to get out of the delightful experience of some Podunk little sheriff's office. He was not going to be driving the one-of-a-kind Shelby he'd picked up at auction to his friend, Wood, when his task in Montana was done.

Not anytime soon, anyway. The wreck of Wood's car was even now being hauled away.

And third, the woman—Hadley—might be the prettiest female he'd encountered in a long while, but she looked like she'd jump out of her skin if a rabbit so much as looked at her.

Dane Rutherford was no rabbit. He liked to look *and* touch.

He'd be doing neither.

"If you're going to impound the car, there's not much I can do to stop you," he told the sheriff. Not much, *yet.* "But you probably realize that it's in your sister's best interest that we each take care of our own damages." He pulled out his money clip and heard Hadley's soft inhalation.

The sheriff's expression didn't change much, though his gaze focused on the folded bills in Dane's hand. "Hadley," he said without looking at her. "Does your truck still run?"

The woman cast a wary look at Dane, her gaze going in a little triangle between the money, the sheriff's face and Dane. "I don't know."

"Try it. If it does, drive it into town," the sheriff said flatly. "Meet us at the station."

Her soft lips compressed. Even with her nose all pink from the cold, she had the kind of face a man could look at for a while. A long while. "Shane, come on. You're not really—"

"Go."

She looked up at Dane again, her expression seeming apologetic. Rightfully so, he reminded himself, given her terrible driving.

"Hadley." The sheriff's voice was warning.

She exhaled abruptly and turned on her heel, stomping across the highway to the decrepit truck, her slender hips swaying beneath the short pink excuse of a jacket she wore. She climbed up in the cab, ground the gears a few times as she disconnected the truck from the mangled mileage marker, and lumbered off down the road, leaving behind a puff of exhaust.

When Dane looked back at the sheriff, he knew the other man was perfectly aware of where Dane's attention had been.

"Now, then. You want to finish the bribe it looks like you're gearing up to offer, or do you want to tell me what's really going on here?"

Hadley grumbled under her breath as she coaxed her ailing pickup truck all the way into town. She pulled into the lot beside Stu's garage and gathered up all the items that were still strewn across the seat, replacing them in her purse. Then she went into the small office that her brother used when he was in town working at the garage. Some might have thought it odd that Stu Golightly was a rancher *and* ran the town's only auto-body and repair shop. Personally, she considered it a great convenience. And the darned man better not have the nerve to bill her for the repairs, either, since it was his own fault she'd been so preoccupied.

The tow truck bearing the crumpled old convertible was parked near the closed bay door, and she carefully looked away from the wreckage and went inside.

It was nearly quitting time, but Riva was still sitting behind the counter painting her fingernails a putrid shade of blue and didn't even look up until Hadley plopped her keys next to the woman's splayed fingers.

Riva popped her gum, her penciled-in eyebrows lifting. She was seventy if she was a day, but that didn't stop Riva from keeping "fashionable," as she called it.

"Guess you had a little problem today," she observed. "What'd *you* hit?"

Hadley told her. "I'm afraid Stu will be busy with that old car there first, though."

Riva cackled at that and nodded her bright-pink head. "That he will. Your brother's gonna wet his pants when he gets a chance to work on a piece of heaven like that. You probably oughta just go talk to your insurance agent about the claim now. Won't be pretty, I expect."

"Actually, we're handling our own damages," Hadley said, mentally crossing her fingers that this would still be the case. Unless her stubborn brother made Wood mad enough to rescind the offer.

Atwood Tolliver. That definitely could *not* be the name of a car thief, right? It sounded so old-fashioned. So upstanding. And the man himself had seemed so...so—

"You going to stand there and daydream all day?" Riva's voice finally penetrated, and Hadley flushed a little, marshaling her thoughts. "Heard that you pulled right in front of him out near Stu's place."

"Nothing like the Lucius grapevine to get the word spread," Hadley murmured.

"So why's he willing to pay his own damages on a car like that?"

Hadley looked over her shoulder, through the

somewhat grimy window to the tow truck outside. "Like what? That car's even older than my pickup."

Riva snapped her gum and shook her head. "Honey, it is a mystery to me how you can have a brother who knows cars the way he does, and be as oblivious as you are." She poked her nail polish brush back into the bottle, drew out a fresh batch of blue and slid it over her half-inch long nails. "That's a '68 Shelby GT500 convertible. It won't be cheap to fix."

Hadley looked again out the window. Down the street a ways, Shane's SUV had pulled to a stop in front of the sheriff's office. "It's valuable then?" Her voice sounded too weak for her liking, but there wasn't much she could do about it. Besides, she'd known Riva since she was barely out of kindergarten.

"Think they only made 500 or so of them."

Oh. Dear. Hadley's stomach sank. No wonder her brother was leery of Wood. "Shane wanted me to meet him at his office. Guess I'd better go."

Riva looked up at her after she just stood there, though. "Might help some if you open the door, child, and actually move your feet in the right direction."

Hadley smiled weakly and went back out into the late afternoon. Her boots dragged a little as she passed the tow truck. She eyed the lines of the vehicle. Okay, so it was kind of a sexy old car....

If it hadn't been crumpled down by a third of its size, maybe.

She exhaled and hurried her step, jogging across the street. One of the old-fashioned streetlamps flicked on as she passed it. Another hour or so, and it would be dark outside. She quickened her pace. She still had things to take care of at Tiff's.

The bell over Shane's door jingled when she went inside his office. Carla Chapman, Shane's secretary-dispatcher-everything-else jerked her head toward Shane's cubicle behind her. "He's waiting for you," she said.

Great. She loved her brother dearly, but the man had a distinct ability to make her feel as if she were being called down to the principal's office.

It was warm inside and she unbuttoned her jacket, sliding it from her shoulders as she entered Shane's cubicle.

Wood was not sitting in either of the two chairs situated in front of Shane's massive metal desk. She dropped her jacket and purse on the desk and leaned toward him. "You locked him up, didn't you." Her voice was accusing.

He pointedly moved her belongings to one side, off his paperwork. "Sit down. You still need to sign the report."

"That's not an answer."

He lifted an eyebrow. "He's in a cell," he allowed after a moment.

"Shane!" She sat down, dismayed more than was wise. "For not having his driver's license? That's ridiculous. I'm sure he has one, he just didn't have it with him."

"Try bribery, then."

"Bri—" Her voice choked. "He did not."

Her brother shrugged. "Guess he had no room in

his pocket for the license what with all that cash he was carrying,'' Shane said dryly. "And you've always been a trusting little soul."

"Makes me sound like I'm seven instead of twenty-seven." She took the pen he extended and signed her name at the bottom of the accident report. "You haven't locked up everyone who forgot their driver's license at home."

"Fortunately today she learned to take her purse or wallet with her when she left the house." He looked sideways at her purse, assuring her that, *yes*, he was referring to her.

Darn his memory, anyway.

"You're being unreasonable."

He sat back and propped one boot heel over his knee. "Our Mr. Tolliver's got quite the public defender in you." The toe of his boot tapped the air twice. "Wonder why?"

"Look. If Stu...and *you*...weren't so determined to hitch me to Wendell Pierce's wagon, none of this would have happened. That poor man would have driven right through Lucius on his way to, to wherever, and that would be that. He was just an—"

"Innocent bystander," Shane put in, amused.

"Yes!"

He dropped his foot back to the floor and sat forward, arms on the desk. His amusement faded. "Doesn't work that way, turnip. Until I know that car's not stolen, he's not going anywhere."

She eyed him, but knew there was no moving Shane when his mind was set. "Dad says that stubbornness is *not* a blessing."

"Dad says a lot of things," Shane agreed mildly.

Frustrated, she snatched up her belongings and turned on her heel.

"Where are you going?"

"Back to see your poor prisoner!" She strode down the tiled hallway. The Lucius Sheriff Office housed a total of five cells and it was a rare day when even one was called into use. Shane was probably just bored and wanted to test the strength of the iron bars or something.

She turned the corner and stopped. Her breath sucked back up into her chest and a squiggle of something unfamiliar dipped in her stomach. Wood was sitting on the cot, his back against the wall, one foot planted on the thin mattress, the other leg—a long leg—extended.

"If you've come to break me out, save the effort," he advised. "With your help I'd probably find myself in a federal penitentiary."

She chewed the inside of her lip and took a step closer to the cell. From out in the front office, she could hear Carla talking on the phone, her voice bright and cheerful.

Just another day winding down in Lucius.

"I'm sorry." She hugged her jacket and purse to her midriff. "This is all my fault."

"Yeah."

"Well," she added after a moment, "it's not my fault that you didn't have your license on you." His lips twisted a little at that. He had very nice lips, even if her brother figured he was a car thief. "Are you?"

His eyebrows rose. "Am I what?"

Her cheeks warmed. That was the trouble for thinking half one's thoughts out loud. Confusion inevitably ensued. "A car thief."

A glint lit his eyes. His hand, draped over his raised knee, curled a little. Then he shifted and rose off the cot, his movements so smooth and relaxed he might just as well have been rising out of his own bed in his own home.

As if she'd ever seen what a strange man looked like rising out of his own bed? She ran the family's boardinghouse. Any beds she was involved with were those needing a change of sheets between her rare guests.

She swallowed and stood her ground when he walked up to the bars of the cell and wrapped his hands lightly around them, looking at her through the space between. "Do I look like a car thief to you?"

She lifted her shoulder. "Can't say I know what a car thief really looks like," she admitted, speculation aside. "I don't imagine they are all unattractive with shifty eyes."

The corner of his lip twisted upward. "High praise," he murmured.

He almost had a dimple in his cheek. Or more of a slash, she thought, which definitely went with a jaw that was razor sharp. And his nose was a little too long for his face, but the whole package was put together in a decidedly blessed way.

"You're staring."

She blinked. Moistened her lips. "Sorry."

He reached one long arm between the bars and grazed his fingers against her coat. "So am I."

He had a tiny scar at the corner of his eye. And another one, nearly invisible, bisecting his slashing eyebrow. "For what?" she asked faintly.

He hooked his finger in a fold of pink wool and tugged lightly.

She looked down. Right. The bloodstains on her jacket. More on the edge of her sweater sleeve. "Cleaning these stains will be a lot easier than fixing your car, I'm afraid."

"So, at least *you've* decided that the Shelby is my car."

How had he gotten those tiny little scars? Would he have a scar when the cut on his forehead healed? "Is there some reason to doubt it?"

He cocked his head a little, considering her. "You're pretty trusting."

For some reason she found herself smiling when the observation came from him. "Surprising, I know, but you are not the first to accuse me of that."

"I'll bet." Lines crinkled at the corner of his eyes, and the tiny scar disappeared.

He wasn't quite smiling but she still felt the impact, and for a moment the metal bars of the cell, the chirping of Carla's voice from out front, everything else disappeared.

"It's getting late. Don't you have to get supper on or something?"

Hadley nearly jumped out of her skin at the sound of her brother's voice.

The cell bars were back.

Wood's hand slowly fell away from her jacket and she looked over her shoulder at Shane. His eyes were hard.

She very nearly argued with him that she had nothing more pressing to do than stand there staring at the man in the cell. Well, the brave little part of her that occasionally snuck past her larger sissy part nearly argued with him. But the truth was, she did have to get supper started. And after that, she needed to mix up bread dough for the rolls she'd bake first thing in the morning, and she had to get the tower room prepared for a guest coming the next day.

Staying wasn't an option, even if she could have summoned the nerve to flout Shane.

Wood moved away from the cell bars and sat down on the cot, back propped against the wall again. He ran the tip of his index finger over the edge of the adhesive on his forehead.

She wondered what he was thinking and she wondered over the fact that had her brother not been standing there acting all Cro-Magnon, she would have actually asked Wood. And wasn't that a surprise? Maybe if she pretended she were a fearless heroine, set on freeing the misunderstood hero, she'd manage to pull it off.

Or not.

"You better feed him," she hissed as she passed Shane. "And give him some aspirin or something for his head. Better yet, call in a doctor. For all you know, he could have a concussion."

"Mr. Tolliver's gonna get everything he deserves," Shane assured.

Ordinarily that would have been a comforting statement. In this situation, however? She grimaced and left, casting one last look at Shane's prisoner.

He wasn't looking at her, this time. He was staring down her brother across the distance of the cell, and even though he *was* behind bars, Hadley couldn't help but wonder which of the two men would come out on top.

She pulled on her stained jacket and went back outside, waving to Carla, who was still jabbering on the phone. The sun had begun to set. Lights were glowing from the window fronts of the businesses along Main. The snow had stopped for the moment, and everything was covered with a thin veil of perfect white powder.

Including the wreck she could easily see from where she stood, still sitting atop the Finns' tow truck.

Wrapping her jacket more tightly around her, she hurried in the opposite direction toward the boarding-house. She could have gone by the church to get a ride from her dad. He'd have undoubtedly still been there. But since it was nearly as far a walk to Beau Golightly's home-away-from home as it was to Tiff's, there seemed little point.

Besides. She wasn't quite ready to find out whether or not her dad had been in on her brothers' ganging up on her over Wendell.

Her face felt stiff with cold and her hands were completely numb by the time she climbed the wide porch steps leading to the front door of the aging Victorian. But inside, the air was warm and welcoming. From the parlor, she could hear someone tinkering on the piano. Probably Mrs. Ardelle. She regularly insisted that she was musical, but—so far—hadn't proved it by the way she attacked the keys.

Still, Mrs. Ardelle was a darling soul, and if she wanted to pretend she could play, who was Hadley to stop her?

She hung up her jacket on the coat tree in the wide hall and walked through to the kitchen, located at the rear of the house. The ever-present coffee was hot so she poured herself a mug before getting down to preparing dinner. Her residents didn't join her in the dining room for dinner every night. They were all welcome—for a fee, of course, which Hadley charged only because her sister tended to get on her case when she didn't—but usually one or two showed up.

Fortunately, cooking for a handful of people was mindlessly familiar to Hadley, and by the time they sat down around the oval walnut table in the dining room, the resulting meal was perfectly edible and showed no sign that Hadley had fretted her way right through preparing it.

In the morning, after she'd baked up a batch of sticky cinnamon rolls and cranberry walnut muffins, she prepared a small picnic basket and walked back downtown to Shane's office.

The door was unlocked. Carla wasn't at her desk yet, but she could plainly hear her brother's voice coming from his cubicle in the back, so she walked right through.

His eyes perked up at the sight of the cloth-covered basket in her mittened hands, and he waved her over to the chairs. A good sign. Shane had always had a soft spot for her rolls.

She set the basket on his desk and sat down, busying herself with tugging off her mittens and unwinding her red scarf from the collar of her serviceable blue parka while he finished his phone call.

"So, you *are* still speaking to me." He reached for the basket.

She nimbly slid the basket out of his reach. "Have you come to your senses and let that poor man go?"

"If I haven't, you think I'm going to change my mind through *your* bribery attempts?"

"I'm sure he didn't really try to bribe you."

He folded his arms across the top of his desk. "Are you, now?"

She had a moment's pause. She had no idea *what* might have transpired between Shane and Wood when she wasn't around.

Then she thought of those intensely blue eyes that had occupied her dreams the entire night. "Yes. I am sure."

He eyed her, shook his head and sat back. "Fine. As it happens, I've let—"

"Good morning."

Hadley jumped a little and turned her head. Wood stood behind them. His hair was darkly damp and falling over his forehead as if he'd just showered, and it partially obscured the fresh bandage there. He'd also replaced his bloodstained shirt with a royal blue one she distinctly remembered giving Shane two

Christmases earlier. "Good…morning." Speech was hard when her breath was caught in her throat.

Shane grabbed a large manila envelope and held it toward Wood. "Check the contents and sign the report. Bus leaves for Billings in about thirty minutes. I'll drive you over."

"You're leaving? But what about your car?" She looked from Wood to her brother. She was glad Shane was being more reasonable about holding Wood, but she couldn't say the same thing at all about the prospect of the man leaving so quickly.

And wasn't that ridiculous? He was a stranger, just passing through. A victim of her preoccupied driving, for pity's sake. Of course he wants to get the heck out of Lucius. The silent thought mocked her.

Shane gave the phone a glare when it started ringing. "His car'll be fixed whether he's in town or not."

Wood had upended the envelope over the side of Shane's desk. A narrow leather wallet. The wad of bills, held by a silver clip engraved with a race car disappeared in the front pocket of his black jeans. Then he flipped open his wallet, looked inside, flipped it closed and pocketed it, as well, before scratching his name across the form Shane had indicated and shrugging into his leather bomber jacket.

And still Shane's phone rang. "I'll give him a lift to the bus station," she offered suddenly. "Better answer that. Carla's not out front."

"She called in sick."

"All the more reason for me to give Mr. Tolliver

a ride. It's the least I can do,'' she added hurriedly when Shane shook his head.

"Appreciate it.'' Wood picked up her scarf and handed it to her, as if the decision were made.

She didn't look at her brother as she tucked her fingers into her mittens and preceded Wood out of the cubicle. Behind her, she heard Shane pick up the phone, growling a greeting.

"He's usually more pleasant in the mornings,'' Hadley whispered. She had to curtail the urge to run out of the office before she crumbled to Shane's displeasure.

Wood reached out and opened the door. The bell jingled softly. "He's protective of you.''

As soon as they stepped out on the sidewalk, Hadley realized that she didn't have the means to even *give* Wood Tolliver a ride to the bus depot. Because her truck was still over at Stu's garage.

Embarrassed beyond belief, she looked up at him. "He's had a lot of practice, I'm afraid. Of being protective, I mean. I, um, I forgot one detail.'' The fringed ends of her scarf skipped around in the breeze. "My keys are across the street at the garage. And Riva—she kind of manages the place for my brother—won't be there for another hour at least.'' She felt like an utter fool, which was something she ought to be used to, considering she'd been feeling foolish since she'd run him off the road. "I'll tell Shane he should take you. I can answer his phones while he's out.'' She reached for the door.

Wood closed his hand over hers and she jumped.

His eyes narrowed a little and he let go. "Are you afraid of me?"

"No! No, of course not." She pressed her hands together. She was not so stupid that she'd tell him she'd felt a *zing* right through the fluffy red mitten when he'd touched her hand. He'd probably laugh right out loud at her. "I'm not afraid of anyone." Which wasn't strictly true if she thought about it. "And Lucius isn't big, but walking all the way out to the bus depot would take too long, so—"

"I don't want to go to the bus depot. Is there a café around here or something?"

"Yes, of course. But Shane—"

"Doesn't much like strangers in his town. He made that abundantly clear." He toyed with the fringe of her scarf that had blown across his sleeve. "The burger your sheriff gave me last night was okay, but I haven't had a full meal since yesterday morning. I'm starving."

And she couldn't seem to draw in a normal breath. "The Luscious Lucius has the best waffles around."

"Luscious," he murmured softly. "Interesting name. Any other restaurants?"

"Sure. But Luscious is the best for breakfast. And lunch."

"And dinner?"

"The Silver Dollar. I know the owner."

"I'll bet you know everyone in town."

"Not quite, but close." She didn't know how they'd come to be standing so closely. She could smell the clean scent of soap on him and it was definitely affecting her thought processes. "Sort of comes with my dad being a minister at the largest church in town and my brother being the sheriff.'' She swallowed and reached past him, pointing down the street. ''Luscious is right over there. See the sign? It's kind of small.''

He lifted the ends of her scarf and slowly looped them together. ''It's cold out.''

She nodded hesitantly. The truth was, her skin felt as though it was being melted from the inside. ''If you miss the bus this morning, there'll be another one late this afternoon. Tomorrow's Saturday, though, and there's only that last run until Monday.''

''I couldn't care less what the bus schedule is, to-day or tomorrow.''

''I thought you wanted to leave.''

''Your brother wants me to leave.'' His knuckles brushed her jaw as he tucked the soft red knit closely around her neck. ''*I* want breakfast.''

She swallowed. ''D-did you steal that car?''

He slowly shook his head. Just once. ''I even plan to pay for my waffle.''

She couldn't help smiling back when his lips tilted. ''And you didn't try to bribe Shane.''

''Your brother doesn't strike me as a man who can be bought.''

''He isn't.''

''Glad we've got that settled.'' He glanced over his shoulder to watch a car creep down Main. It turned and parked in front of the café. ''Somebody else going after those waffles, I suppose.'' He took a step in that direction, then stopped and looked back at her. He lifted one eyebrow, his intensely blue eyes definitely amused. ''Well? You coming or not?''

Chapter Three

She was right. The waffles at the Luscious Lucius Café were better than average.

Or maybe it was the company sitting across the table from him that made the waffles taste better than usual. Dane's reason for being in Montana had nothing to do with pleasure, but he wasn't going to look a gift horse in the mouth.

Despite her questionable skills behind the wheel, Hadley Golightly was easy on the eyes, humorous and engaging, when she wasn't busy being self-conscious, and did seem to know everyone in town.

Not a single person entered or left the café without exchanging some friendly greeting with her. He'd been introduced to more people in the past hour than he could have met had he advertised free money. Wood Tolliver had been introduced, anyway.

And Dane figured it was only a matter of time before the sheriff came along, set to hurry him on his way. Once the man had determined that the Shelby *hadn't* been reported stolen, he'd had little reason to keep holding "Wood." But he'd been clear that he wanted to see the back side of Dane, regardless.

It was a new sensation for him. Most people were happy to have Dane Rutherford in their midst. Came with the territory of running Rutherford Industries.

But Dane wasn't in Montana on business.

This trip had been strictly personal.

Which was why he'd borrowed Wood's name. Tolliver wasn't likely to be recognized. Rutherford, however, was as common as Rockefeller.

And a Rutherford asking questions about new faces in town would draw speculation he didn't need.

He nudged aside his plate and folded his arms on the table, watching Hadley. "You've told me all about Lucius. Tell me about you."

Her eyes were as dark a brown as her hair. And now they widened a little. A hint of pink rode her cheeks, and he knew it was nature that had put it there, not cosmetics. "There's nothing much to tell."

"You have one brother who's the sheriff and one brother who's the mechanic."

"Stu also has a ranch. Outside of town." Her cheeks went a little more pink. "I was leaving there when I—"

"Was driving like a bat outta hell?"

She poked the tines of her fork into her waffle and nodded.

"And Wendell Pierce?"

Her eyes flickered. "What do you know about Wendell?"

"Your brother says you two are involved."

Her jaw worked. She carefully set down the fork. "I can't imagine why he'd say that."

Dane could. Shane-the-sheriff didn't like the way Dane looked at his kid sister.

He couldn't really blame the guy for that, he supposed.

"Maybe I misunderstood," he lied smoothly.

"I doubt it," she muttered. Her brown gaze skipped around the café. Half the tables and all of the booths were occupied. Then she leaned forward. "They're trying to marry me off," she said abruptly. "I mean, do I look that pathetic to you?" She shook her head, and her hair rippled over the turtleneck she wore. It was a pretty, soft yellow. And at least a size too large.

"Never mind," she hurried onward. "Don't answer that. My ego can only take so much."

Her ego should have been plenty healthy. Either the men in Lucius—excluding the apparently interested Wendell—were terminally stupid, or they were blind. And he figured that he'd been better off thinking she was already spoken for in the romance department.

He wasn't in Montana for romance. Or for good old-fashioned lust, which was definitely a shame, because she certainly inspired that, even with her engulfing sweater.

Hardly a polite topic over breakfast dishes, though,

and Dane had been schooled from way back about what was polite and what was not. Seemly behavior versus unseemly.

Not that he'd ever paid those lessons much heed.

"I have a sister," he said truthfully. "Before she got married a while back I was guilty of derailing a few interested men that I didn't think were good enough for her."

"But that's not what they're doing." She lifted her hands. "They're trying to tie me to the tracks, because they know that nobody besides Wendell *is* interested."

He couldn't help smiling a little, she was so clearly irritated. Telling her that, where he was concerned, her thinking was completely off the mark would only lead to trouble, so he just reached for his mug and finished off his coffee.

She sat back in her chair again and finally set down the fork with which she'd been doing more waving than eating. "The accident *was* my fault," she said. "You shouldn't have to pay for your own damages. I have insurance." Her expression was earnest. "And Stu may be a pain in my behind, but he's really a whiz when it comes to fixing cars. He keeps this whole town running, pretty much. And he makes things so beautiful again. Or maybe you want to have your car hauled back to where you live in Indiana?"

He hadn't spent more than five days straight in Indiana for the past decade, and he could have had an entire team come to Lucius to work on the car he'd picked up on Wood's behalf if he'd wanted. "A whiz, huh?"

The shining ends of her hair bounced around the barely discernible thrust of her breasts when she nodded. "Honest."

"Guess I'll have to look into it, then."

Her smile lit every portion of her face, including her eyes. Then she looked at her watch. "Oh, drat. I've got to go. I've been helping my dad out mornings for a few weeks at the church while his secretary is on vacation. If you're going to be staying in town, let me know. I run Tiff's. It's the boardinghouse at the end of Main Street. Can't miss the place." She fumbled some cash out of her purse, dropped it on the table and had scurried out the door before he could get a word out.

Dane sat back in his chair once more and eyed her money.

He couldn't remember the last time he hadn't been expected to pick up the check, no matter how large or small. And with the women he usually saw, the check had never involved waffles in a quaint café with a western-style front on a quiet street that saw maybe three cars an hour.

The busy waitress—Bethany, according to her hand-printed nametag—came by with the coffee pot, and he slid his mug toward her. She filled it, offered a distracted smile and headed on to the next table. The people at the tables around him discussed everything from the uncommonly cold weather, to politics, to who was apparently sleeping with whom. And they acted as if he had every reason to be included.

Even though he'd spent the night in a jail cell, now

he'd been introduced by Hadley Golightly. Apparently that was enough. It also made her glad he hadn't pulled any strings to get out of jail from the get-go. He was nothing more than a guy passing through.

Eventually Dane finished off the coffee. More in hopes that it would help the throbbing in his head than anything. The morning crowd had thinned and he pocketed Hadley's cash and paid the full bill himself. Then he walked down to Golightly Garage and Auto Body. The Shelby had been moved from the tow truck and was parked in front of an open bay.

For a moment Dane let himself suck in the stink of tires and grease. It had been a long time.

Too long.

He shook off the thought with regrettably practiced ease and walked forward when the man circling the car with a clipboard in his hand noticed him.

The other man lifted a square palm and settled his Green Bay Packers ball cap a few inches back on his blond head. "You Tolliver?"

Dane nodded. The other man stepped forward, hand extended and they shook. "Stu Golightly." He gestured at the car with his other hand, which was encased in a ragged cast. "Damn, but this is a pure shame. Guess you met my little sister, Had, eh?"

Hadley had told him over breakfast that Shane and Stu were twins, but aside from their general size— extra large—there was little resemblance. "She tells me you're a whiz."

Stu grinned, apparently as friendly as his brother

was not. "I am, but I 'spect you'll have someone you prefer to work on her."

He did. But that didn't serve his purposes at all.

He went around and pried open the passenger door wide enough to pull his leather duffel from where it was wedged behind the seat, along with the driver's license he'd stashed in a tight fold of leather upholstery the day before when the ambulance had arrived. He stuck the license in his pocket and backed out of the car.

"Write up the estimate," he told the man, "and call me. I assume you know the number at Tiff's."

Stu's friendly expression chilled. Seemed he was more like his brother than Dane had thought. "You're staying at Tiff's?"

Dane nodded and walked away before the man could say more. Judging by that expression, Stu would have the repairs done on the Shelby in record time. The guy may have been happy to work on the rare car, but his enthusiasm evidently didn't extend to the idea of Dane taking a room at his sister's boardinghouse.

By the time he'd walked the length of Main Street, Dane had a renewed appreciation for warmer climates. Not that it didn't get cold in Seattle or Louisville, where he had homes. But it was nothing compared to the chip of ice Lucius occupied.

Fortunately, Tiff's was just as Hadley had described. The Victorian looked perfectly maintained with its curlicues and lace. But it was painted in pink and green, resulting in what was about the most godawful color combination Dane had ever seen.

He went up the front steps. As long as it was warm inside, he didn't much care if there were naked ladies painted on the outside. The door was unlocked and he went in, not entirely sure what to expect. He was used to staying in five-star hotels. Not Podunk-town boardinghouses.

The door opened directly on to a wide hall with several doorways leading off it. The floor was carpeted in a pale pink as ugly as the exterior paint, and a narrow tapestry carpet runner stretched along the length of it. Looking straight back, beyond the dark-wood staircase tucked against the wall, he could see what was obviously a kitchen.

And the painstaking piano music coming from one of the rooms off the central hall seemed completely in place.

"Hi." A very pregnant young blonde walked by, an enormous cereal bowl in her hand. "You must be the new guest."

Why not? He nodded, and the woman pointed up the stairs. "All the way up the stairs. Two flights. Tower room. You're lucky. You'll have your own bathroom." Then she padded, barefoot, out of sight again.

He went up the stairs to the first landing, glanced down the hall at the collection of doors—mostly closed, and went up the second flight. There was only one room at the top and he went inside, closing the door behind him.

There were windows on three sides of the room. All were covered with filmy white curtains, and Dane tugged aside one set to look out on a wide expanse of snow punctuated periodically by winter-nude trees. In the distance he could see the thin, glittering ribbon of a stream backed by a row of evergreens.

He shrugged out of his coat and retrieved his cell phone from his duffel. As soon as he turned it on, it beeped with messages. He ignored them and dialed his sister. She answered after only a few rings.

Dane didn't waste time. "How is he?"

"Stable for now," Darby answered.

"Still unconscious?"

"Yes."

Dane stifled an oath. "Is Felicia there?"

Darby laughed a little at that. "Are you kidding? Our mother doesn't *do* hospitals, you know that. Not even for our dad. She's staying at the house, though."

"If Roth knew she was staying under his roof, he'd probably have another heart attack," he said. Once Roth and Felicia Rutherford divorced, they'd never had another kind word to say about the other.

More than twenty years ago, yet neither one of his parents had managed to move on.

He gingerly rubbed the pain in his forehead and turned away from the view.

He was a fine one to judge others about moving on.

"Call me on my cell if anything changes."

Darby promised to do so and hung up. She'd never have bought it if he'd claimed to be taking a vacation and it had been easy enough to convince her he was in Montana on business. Her interest in Rutherford Industries had always been minimal, and since she now lived in Minnesota with her husband, the five kids he'd come with plus the one they'd had together, that interest had decreased even further.

Only, now Darby was back in Louisville, staying by Roth's hospital bedside. He knew she didn't approve of him being absent right now even if she understood it to be business. But it was better if she didn't know Dane's real reason.

His sister had been through enough when it came to Dane's quarry. Alan Michaels had kidnapped and tormented her when she was a child. He had no intention of telling her that the man was at large again. Hell, Roth had suffered a heart attack the same day *he'd* learned it.

Dane looked around the room. It wasn't going to win any awards for spacious design, but it had the necessities and was appealing in a comfortable sort of way with its clean, light looks. The bed was wide enough, covered by a quilt that he figured was handmade, and there was a narrow desk and chair beneath the set of windows that overlooked the street.

He ached from head to toe and the bed looked inviting, but he had work to do. So he sat down in the chair and dealt with the phone messages. He called Wood and broke the news about the car. His friend mostly groaned. But since Wood already had three other Shelbys in his collection, he could afford the luxury of being patient for the repairs. Then Dane called Mandy Manning. The message he left on her voice mail was brief.

"I'm in Lucius. Call me."

* * *

"I'm late, I'm late for a very important date." The words echoed inside Hadley's head as she hurried up the steps of Tiff's. She'd spent an hour longer than she'd intended at the church, and had still had to stop off at the grocery store before going home.

Since sharing a table at Luscious with Wood Tolliver that morning, it'd taken her twice as long to accomplish everything she'd attempted, because her thoughts kept straying into foolish directions.

She'd mangled his car and that was that. She didn't figure a man would be likely to overlook that particular detail.

She maneuvered the front door open with her two free fingertips, worked a foot inside, followed by her thigh, then hip.

"Here."

She nearly jumped out of her skin when Wood seemed to appear out of nowhere on the step beside her, his hands easily plucking three of the bulky canvas bags out of her hands.

"Where do you want them?"

"Kitchen," she said faintly. He was polite enough not to mention her gaping expression, and she was grateful for it.

He pushed open the door the rest of the way for her and waited. She could feel cold air rushing past her and she hurriedly closed her mouth and went inside.

He followed her into the kitchen and set his bags on the counter next to hers. Then she tried not to gape all over again when he tossed his jacket on the counter and—as if he'd been doing it for years—

poured himself a mug of coffee. Well, she tried and failed, anyway, and managed to shake her head when he held up the mug, offering it to her first before lifting it to his own lips.

"You look surprised," he said after a moment. He leaned his hip against the counter and smiled faintly. "Is it me drinking your coffee, or is it just me?"

Her oversize white mugs were eclipsed by his long fingers. His nails were clipped short and neat and she couldn't imagine there ever being grease or dirt beneath them. He'd also changed out of the borrowed shirt, she noticed, and the gray one he now wore made his blue eyes seem less piercing but no less…arresting.

"I am," she admitted belatedly. "Surprised you're here, I mean." The Lucius grapevine must have had a temporary power outage.

"Should I have gone elsewhere? You're the one who suggested it."

She had, in a minor fit of madness even though she'd never believed he would take her up on it. "The Lucius Inn might be more to your liking. They have room service, and satellite television and—"

"Now you're making me feel unwelcome."

"No!" Dismayed, her fingers crumpled the canvas bag she'd been unpacking. "I didn't mean that at all. Of course you're welcome here. It's the least I can do. But, I just—"

"Hadley."

"What?"

He set his mug down and leaned his arms on the

counter until his face was only a foot from hers. "I was kidding."

She could see those small scars near his eye again. "Oh. Right."

His mouth kicked up a little on one side and after a moment he straightened again, picking up the mug. "Got a lot of stuff there. Thought you were helping out your dad at his church this morning."

She swallowed and diligently focused again on unpacking her purchases. "I was. I did. Then I went shopping." Nothing like stating the obvious, Hadley. Her face felt hot. "I have another guest coming in this afternoon. She actually made the reservation a few weeks ago, which is pretty unusual for me. So I wanted to make it particularly special for her."

Wood lifted a tissue-wrapped bundle of wild flowers from the smallest bag. "Nice." He tipped the bundle toward his nose, smelling them. "You buy flowers for all your guests?"

Feeling like the biggest ninny on the planet, she cautiously slipped them out of his hand. "Not for the regulars." If she were one of her characters that she wrote about, she'd have flirted outrageously with the man and had him falling over himself to win her heart.

Instead she retrieved a crystal vase from the breakfront and filled it with water, wishing that she could control the heat that filled her cheeks whenever she glanced his way.

He had to move out of her way for her to reach the sink, which he did, but not enough, and standing so near to him made her breath feel woefully short.

"Tiff's used to really be a bed and breakfast, but since I've taken over we've become more of a boardinghouse." She turned off the water and reached for the flowers again.

"Who ran it before you?"

"My mother, Holly."

His eyebrows rose. "Holly. Golightly."

His surprise was toned down more than the usual disbelief she'd heard most of her life and she found herself smiling a little. "I know. And, yes, her favorite movie was *Breakfast at Tiffany's* with Audrey Hepburn. Mom wasn't anything like the character Holly Golightly, though. Well, other than being a survivor." She arranged the flowers and stepped back to study them.

"Pretty," he murmured.

She nodded, her eyes still on the flowers.

"What happened to her?"

Hadley sighed a little. "She died when I was twenty. Cancer."

"I'm sorry."

Funnily enough, she had the sense the words weren't merely a platitude. She looked up at him and he wasn't looking at the flowers, at all. "We all were." And even though there were days she missed her mother with a physical ache, she'd lived through the worst of her grief and could think about her without wanting to dissolve.

She set the flowers safely to one side and returned to unpacking the rest of her purchases. Any minute he'd probably get bored and leave the room. "What about your parents?'' she asked quickly, before she lost her nerve.

"Divorced a long time ago."

She paused, caught by something in his expression that she couldn't have defined had she tried. "That must have been hard," she said quietly.

His gaze didn't waver. "Be glad you never had to live through your own parents going to war."

Hadley's fingers tightened around a fresh tomato. She set it down before she punctured the skin. The war between her mother and natural father had gone on before she'd been born. Beau Golightly was her stepfather. "So." She took a cheerful note. "What's the word on your car?"

"Your brother is working up the estimate."

"He'll be fair. And not just in deference to my insurance rates that are undoubtedly going to go up again."

"Again?"

She shrugged and smiled ruefully. What was the point in being offended over the simple truth? She folded the emptied canvas bags and stacked them beneath the sink. "We both know I'm not going to win any driving awards." She straightened and brushed her hands down her slacks.

Maybe if she focused on the business at hand, she would prove she wasn't inept in that area, at least. "We need to get you settled in a room, then. Can't have you just hovering around the downstairs rooms with no place of your own."

Joanie Adams padded into the kitchen, the ever-present cereal bowl in her young hand. "No sweat,

Had,'' she said, obviously overhearing Hadley's comment. ''I told him to go up to the tower room. He's the one you were expecting, right?''

Hadley's smile wilted a little. Joanie had her heart in the right place. ''Actually, he isn't.''

Joanie's sweet face fell. ''Oh, I'm so sorry.''

Hadley waved her hands. ''Don't be silly. I should have been here when Mr. Tolliver arrived. It'll all be fine.''

''I'm not choosy,'' Wood murmured. ''As long as there's a bed.''

But Joanie still looked troubled. Fat tears filled her blue eyes. ''I was only trying to help.''

Hadley tucked her arm through Joanie's, leading her from the kitchen. She knew from experience that once Joanie started the waterworks, it only got worse from there. ''I know you were,'' she soothed. ''Truly, Joanie. It's fine. No harm done.'' She snuck an apologetic look over her shoulder at Wood as she herded Joanie back to her room. If he thought Joanie's reaction extreme, it didn't show on his face.

The man was proving to have the patience of Job.

The only other person she knew personally with that kind of patience was her stepfather, Beau.

By the time Hadley had opened a fresh box of tissues and Joanie's wailing had ceased, Hadley wanted nothing more than to sit down with a good book and put up her feet. But lunch needed to be prepared, and she had to move Wood out of the tower and into the only other room she had prepared for guests.

Mrs. Ardelle was banging away on the piano keys,

and Hadley stuck her head in the parlor, meaning to yell hello over the notes.

Wood sat on the bench beside the white-haired woman, holding the pages of the sheet music in place.

Hadley hovered, unnoticed in the doorway until Mrs. Ardelle finished with a flourish and dimpled at Wood. "Do you play?"

He lifted a shoulder. "Badly. Blame six years of enforced lessons. No—" he waved Mrs. Ardelle back in place on the bench when she made to move so he could take her spot "—you keep playing. My ego would roll over and die if I made an attempt at it."

Mrs. Ardelle laughed gaily, clearly taken with Wood's deprecatory drawl. Hadley smiled herself as she tiptoed back to the kitchen without disturbing the two.

Fortunately, lunch was easy, requiring little of her thoughts, which were definitely preoccupied again with her unexpected guest. Chicken salad, broccoli soup and pecan tarts. When everything was ready she set it all out on the buffet in the dining room using special containers that would keep the dishes hot or cold, and rang the dinner bell. They'd come by and eat when it suited them over the next hour.

Wood escorted Mrs. Ardelle into the dining room before Hadley escaped to spend her lunchtime as she usually did—squirreled away in her room for an uninterrupted hour of writing. But she surprised everyone, including herself, by fixing herself a serving and sitting down at the table.

Mrs. Ardelle's bright eyes skipped from Wood to

her as she chattered about the latest gossip going around Lucius, and Hadley had the suspicion that she'd just given the elderly woman a new topic to gossip about.

The presence of Wood Tolliver at Tiff's.

Vince Jeffries ambled in. Next to Wood, who didn't really count, Vince was her newest boarder. Typically quiet, the thirty-something balding man sat at the end of the table, barely nodding a greeting at the rest. Even Joanie came in after a fashion, keeping a wide berth between herself and Wood, as if he had been barking at her for the room mix-up when nothing could have been further from the truth.

Hadley couldn't help wondering what he thought of his lunch companions and was no closer to a conclusion when the pecan tarts had all been eaten and the dining room was clear again, save the dirty dishes, her and Wood.

She tried waving him back when he began helping her clear the table, but he paid no heed, and in less than half the time it usually took, she had the dining room restored to order and the kitchen sink was full of soapy water.

"A lot of service you're providing for a boardinghouse," Wood observed.

She gave up protesting his help. The man seemed set on it regardless of what she said. "You're pretty determined to do whatever you want, aren't you?" She looked pointedly at the dish towel he'd picked up.

"Pretty much," he allowed smoothly.

She smiled despite herself and shoved her hands

back in the hot, soapy water. "So, what do you do back in Indiana?"

He dried a plate and carefully stacked it on top of the others. "This and that. What time is your special guest coming this afternoon?"

Hadley glanced up at the clock, dismayed to see how quickly the time was slipping past. "A few hours yet. She said to expect her around four. She's coming up from Wyoming."

He lifted his eyebrows at that, and Hadley shrugged. "From one snowy place to another. I know. But it's business, and believe me, if I turn it away, I'll hear about it from my sister, Evie. She's on my case enough as it is for being too, well, too—"

"Soft?"

She looked sideways at him and felt her heart skid around in her chest again when their gazes met. "Yes."

Steely blue roved over her and she felt it like a physical thing. "Soft isn't necessarily bad," he murmured.

Her face felt warm, and blaming it on the sudsy water would be an outright lie. "Well." Her voice was even more breathless. "It is when the profit margin around here is as minimal as it is. She'd have this place listed on one of those *Best of* shows on television, if she were in charge, and never let any rooms go empty for long."

He slipped the forgotten plate out of her fingers and ran it through the rinse water. "But you don't run Tiff's for the profit, do you."

She blinked, trying to gather her scattered wits, few as they seemed. "When my mother died, my father and brothers wanted me to take over Tiff's. Nobody could bear to sell it off. Evie was already married with her own responsibilities, and there was nobody left but me."

"And what did *you* want?"

"To run Tiff's, of course," she said after a tiny hesitation that she assured herself wasn't noticeable.

He looked back at the dishes he was drying, and she had to resist the impulse to gasp in a breath of air. The man had a serious impact on people. She wondered if he knew.

From beneath her lowered lashes, she watched his movements. He'd rolled up the sleeves of his casual shirt to his elbows and she might not know the names of the latest Paris designers, but she did know silk when she saw it. And the heavy watch circling his corded brown wrist looked like something that never needed an advertisement.

Who was she kidding? Of course he knew his own effect.

"So what's Joanie's problem?" he whispered.

Hadley's tone turned tart. "Other than being eight months pregnant by a good-for-nothing liar who made sure he beat down whatever self-confidence she had left after her father had already stomped out most of it?"

Then, because she was in no mood to let Joanie's ex-boyfriend sour her afternoon, she shook her head and grabbed the last of the bowls. "Sorry. I just cannot abide liars. Anyway, you certainly charmed

Mrs. Ardelle. I haven't seen her smile so much since she moved in here last year after her husband passed away.''

Dane listened to Hadley's determinedly cheerful voice. She couldn't abide liars. Ordinarily he'd have said the same. "And Vince Jeffries?''

"He's been here a few months. He's looking for work.''

"You take in strays.''

Her head swiveled around to look at him, her soft lips parted.

Soft-looking lips. Soft woman.

His fingers strangled the dish towel for a minute. Had it not been for Marlene, the Rutherford family housekeeper, he wouldn't have known one towel from another, much less what to do with it around a pile of dishes. But Marlene hadn't cared that he was Roth Rutherford's heir and had assigned chores whenever it suited her.

"Everybody needs a place to call home,'' Hadley said after a moment. With a quick jerk, she pulled the plug and the soapy water gurgled down the drain. "If Tiff's provides that, then I'm happy.'' She wiped down the counters, rinsed her hands and plucked the dish towel out of Dane's hands. She stood close enough that he could smell the fragrance of her shampoo. It was clean and soft.

Just like she was.

"Come on,'' she said. "We'll get you settled in your new room.''

There was a touch of huskiness in her voice that he was smart enough to take as a warning. She might be useful for his purposes right now, but he didn't tangle with innocent women.

They were too easily hurt.

He nodded and followed her past the staircase and around to the far side of the house. "I'm afraid you'll have to share a bathroom," she said as she pushed open a door and went inside. She picked up an old-fashioned key from the dresser and handed it to him as he entered. "And believe me, considering how nice you've been about the accident and all, I'd be happy to keep you in the tower, but—"

"I'm no Rapunzel," he murmured.

She flushed a little, glancing at his hair. "Prince Charming, maybe." Then she flushed even brighter. "You'll be warmer down here, so that's one advantage. Did you have any luggage?" Her words came so fast they nearly tumbled over each other.

"A duffel. I'll move it right now. I didn't unpack or anything up there, so you shouldn't have to do much to get ready for your other guest."

"That doesn't matter," she assured him quickly as she stepped back into the hall. As if she weren't comfortable being in his room while he was in it, too. "Except for the regulars, I change the sheets and towels and stuff around here. One more doesn't make much of a difference to me."

It wasn't smart of him to think of Hadley *and* bed sheets. Not when the conceivable reasons for that combination dragged at him in a painfully tantalizing way.

He looked over her head at the door adjacent to his. "That the bathroom?"

She slid her foot backward, putting even more inches between them. It amused him. And relieved him from having to do it himself.

"No, actually." She tucked her hair behind her ears, but the rich brown strands fell forward again almost as quickly. "It's my bedroom. The bathroom we'll be sharing is between the rooms." She ducked her head and mumbled an excuse before darting up the hallway. Seconds later he heard a phone ring somewhere in the house, only to be quickly answered.

He eyed the two doors.

Too close together.

Dane scrubbed his hand down his face. Christ.

He was in Montana to settle a score that—in his opinion—could never be settled enough. He didn't have time for distractions.

No matter how beautifully she filled a pair of snug jeans.

Chapter Four

Stu Golightly didn't just phone with the estimate for the repairs to Dane's car. He brought it by himself that evening during dinner. When the man shook his head at Hadley's invitation to stay and eat, Dane excused himself from the dining room table and followed Stu from the room.

The other man didn't stop until he reached the front door, and then he looked as if he'd have preferred to shove Dane through it, than discuss the estimate.

Dane didn't particularly begrudge Stu his attitude any more than he did Shane's. He knew what it was like to feel protective. After all, he was in Montana in the first place because of that very trait. So he looked down the detailed list. "You can get a better deal on the parts. By ten percent, at least."

Stu visibly bristled. "I don't pad my charges."

"I didn't say otherwise. Call—" Damn, he very nearly said Wood Tolliver, and blamed his unusual distractedness on the pain in his head, rather than the brunette who'd been the cause of it. "Call RTM out of Indianapolis. I've done a lot of work with them."

Stu's gaze narrowed, obviously recognizing the name of the company. "They're pretty high end."

R & T Motorworks *was* high end. It was also the business Dane and Wood started when they were in college and making names for themselves on the circuit. Wood may have been in charge of the day-to-day operations for years, now, but Dane still kept his hand in.

Some days he thought it was one of the few ways he stayed sane—focusing on something that *wasn't* part of Rutherford Industries. "Ask for Stephanie," he said. "I'll let her know to expect your call. If she doesn't beat your prices, don't use RTM. Simple enough."

The man looked as if he was trying to come up with an argument. In the end he nodded and settled his ball cap back on his head. "Tell Had that she needs to fill in for Riva on Monday morning." He stepped out the door, hurriedly closing it against the cold evening air.

Dane slowly folded the estimate, tucked it in his pocket and returned to the dining room.

Mrs. Ardelle was chattering away again. The woman never seemed to run out of things to say. In a way she reminded him of Marlene. The new guest, Nikki Day, had arrived shortly before dinner. The auburn-haired newcomer was beautiful and well dressed and probably about Hadley's age, he guessed. She was also pregnant, though not as far along as Joanie. Nikki sat beside her, and he gave the new guest credit for getting Joanie to lighten up enough to actually smile a little. Vince was nowhere to be seen.

Dane sat down again. He was sitting across from Hadley. Suited him. The view of her was as fine as her cooking. "Your brother said Riva needs you to work for her on Monday morning."

She immediately nodded her head.

"Thought you said you'd be filling in at your dad's church in the mornings for a while."

"Right." She passed a platter of roast beef to Joanie, murmuring that the girl needed to eat more protein. "I'll just have to do a few hours at the garage, then a few hours at the church. Hopefully, it won't inconvenience either one of them too much."

Dane wondered if her father or brother had ever considered whether *she'd* be inconvenienced. Not that any of it was his business anyway. He deliberately focused on his meal, letting the various conversations roll over him.

"Wood Tolliver," Mrs. Ardelle said. "The more I think about it, the more that name seems familiar to me, somehow."

Dane smiled noncommittally. Unless she had some insight into the world of custom racing, she wouldn't have been likely to have heard of Wood Tolliver. "Tolliver isn't an unusual name."

Joanie snorted a little at that. "Please. It's not like people call you Bob Smith."

Hadley laughed. Dane looked across at her, smiling despite himself. "I'm not the one with the unusual name," he said. "Not compared to Ms. Golightly here."

"And your mother's name was really Holly?" Nikki Day asked, resting her elbows delicately on the edge of the table. "My, um, I had a friend whose parents stayed here at Tiff's for their wedding night," she explained. "Your mother had just recently opened for business. They were charmed by her."

"Most people were," Hadley agreed. Her gaze flicked to Dane, then she pushed back from the table. "Dessert coming up."

Dane immediately rose to assist her. She looked ready to protest, but obviously had learned her lesson from earlier that day. In the kitchen she arranged the dessert plates on an enormous silver tray and settled pretty crystal cups of chocolate mousse on them.

Marlene couldn't have done better herself, and he knew she'd studied way back when in France. "Your mom teach you to cook?"

Hadley nodded. "And I read cookbooks and stuff. A lot." She grinned, a quick, mischievous little grin that snuck down inside him and plucked hard.

He picked up the heavy tray and jerked his head toward the dining room. "Don't know when you have the time," he said hoping his bluntness would dull the sharp desire he suddenly felt. "Considering how you're always helping out someone else."

She just lifted her shoulders and pushed open the swinging door to the dining room. "They're my family," she said simply.

Dane exhaled and followed her. He loved his sister fiercely. And he loved his mother, though he freely admitted that she was an acquired taste. He loved his stubborn-ass father, too, though Roth had only ever been proud of Dane for the work he'd done at Rutherford Industries.

But he could hardly fathom the simple acceptance that Hadley exhibited.

After dinner Mrs. Ardelle headed for the piano and everyone else headed for their rooms. Dane had plenty of calls stacking up on his voice mail to take care of, but when Hadley pulled on an ancient-looking flannel coat and gloves and said she was going out for a load of wood, he went after her.

"You need to learn the art of relaxing." He yanked on his jacket as he caught up to her in the rear of the house.

She jerked, dropping the split logs she'd selected and pressed her gloved hand to her chest as she turned to see him. "Well, you know what they say. No rest for the wicked. Or something like that."

He snorted softly and picked up the wood she'd dropped. "If there's anything wicked about you, I'll eat this wood."

Her shoulders heaved a little and she leaned over, picking up more logs. "That's kind of my problem, if the truth be known. Everyone in this town knows me."

He was counting on it. "And the problem in that

is what? Wait. Stack those logs on top of mine. You don't need to carry in the wood yourself.''

It was too dark to see her expression, but he felt the amusement in her smile, nonetheless. ''If I don't, who will?''

He hefted the logs a little higher in his arms. ''Hello?''

He could hear bewilderment in her soft laughter. ''You're much too nice to me, given the situation,'' she said.

''Then go out with me.''

She bobbled the logs in her arms again, but saved them from falling. ''I...excuse me?''

''You need to learn how to relax. I know how to relax. I will teach you how to relax. Over a drink. There's gotta be a watering hole in this town somewhere.'' He knew of one, quite specifically.

''Several, but—''

''It's just a drink, Hadley. Your virtue is safe.''

She turned away, muttering something under her breath.

''What was that?''

Her shoulders lifted, then fell. She turned around to face him again. ''I said that was a pity,'' she blurted. ''If I were less virtuous, then maybe Wendell wouldn't be so anxious to fall in with my brothers' plans for me. He's called me four times just this afternoon. Four times! The man doesn't know how to take no for an answer any more than Shane or Stu.''

''So tell them all you're not interested. Nobody can force you to go out with someone you don't want to go out with.''

"Go out with? Oh, believe me. If that were only as far as it goes. I told you before. They want to marry me off, and Wendell Pierce is the intended groom." She shook her head and her dark hair bounced, gleaming in the moonlight. "Wendell knows me from way back. He knows I'm settled and quiet and, and *un*interesting!"

"You settled and quiet?" He couldn't help it. He laughed. "Sweetness, you drive like a bat outta hell, and you have more energy than a swarm of ants."

She eyed him. "Gosh. Flattery indeed." Then, as if she regretted the impulsive words, she ducked her chin and hurried toward the house. Dust and bits of wood rained down from her armload as she went.

Dane was an expert in negotiations. He ran a billion-dollar corporation. He could sure as hell manage not to offend one twenty-something small-town girl, couldn't he?

He found Hadley inside, stacking her wood in the iron bin in one corner of the long kitchen. He crouched down beside her and began unloading his own burden. "I'll make a deal with you."

She dusted her hands together and pushed to her feet, putting distance between them, and he regretted that. It was painfully obvious that—between her spurts of tart humor—he made her nervous.

"What kind of deal?" Her tone was suspicious enough that had her brothers heard it, they'd have applauded.

"I'm going to be stuck in this town for a while. You introduce me around, and if your Wendell gets the wrong idea about you in the process, we'll both be happy."

"Introduce you around to whom? Women?" Her lips twisted. "A man who looks like you doesn't need introductions from *me*." Rosy color filled her cheeks.

It wasn't like him to be sidetracked by anyone, much less a blushing young brunette. "But then Wendell wouldn't get word that your interests might lie elsewhere," he pointed out. "And I didn't say anything about introducing me to other women."

Her eyebrows skyrocketed. "You want me to introduce you to men?"

He exhaled, torn between laughter and aggravation. "People," he clarified. "Just people. Come on, Hadley. I'm a sociable guy." He felt an unexpected pang of conscience at that particularly bald-faced lie. He knew the social games that went along with his place as CEO of Rutherford Industries, but that didn't mean he particularly enjoyed them. "It'll help pass the time while my car's getting fixed. You remember the car, right?"

Remorse filled her eyes. "I'm not likely to forget," she assured.

"Well then." He rose, too, and stepped closer to her. She held her stance, which was surprising, but good. "We go out. Have a few drinks." To please no one but himself, he drew a long lock of hair away from her face and settled it against her wood-dusted flannel shoulder.

Her hair felt just as silky as it looked, and it took

more effort than it should have to move his hand away.

"But...but aren't you tired? You were in an accident yesterday, for pity's sake. You surely don't want to be going out."

"I don't offer to do things if I don't want to. Agree. You learn how to relax," he murmured. "I meet some new people. And maybe your problem with Wendell will solve itself."

Her eyes were impossibly wide. "You talk people into doing lots of things, don't you?"

"Yes." Now *that* was true. Only person he'd never been able to talk into something was Roth.

She exhaled. "I suppose we could go to the Tipped Barrel. It's fairly popular with some people."

The Tipped Barrel was exactly where he wanted to go, only he'd intended to go there alone until Hadley began bemoaning her small difficulty with Wendell.

"And you?"

"Oh, I've never been there. Never been to any bar in my entire life, for that matter. When people see me there, they'll be certain you're corrupting me." A glint sparked in her eyes and she smiled suddenly. Brilliantly. "Okay. I'll do it. Let's go."

"You don't want to change clothes or anything?"

Her enthusiasm visibly faltered and he felt like kicking himself when she looked down at herself. "Right," she muttered. "Of course. How silly of—"

He caught her chin in his fingers and lifted. "You don't *need* to change," he said gruffly. He figured he wouldn't win any awards by telling her he was used to dealing with far more high-maintenance women. "You're perfect the way you are."

She didn't look convinced. And standing there touching her face—satin smooth and velvet soft and, if he wasn't mistaken, completely devoid of artifice—wasn't the smartest thing he'd ever done in his life. Because he definitely wasn't soft. At all.

He lowered his hand. "It's cold out. Do you want to get a warmer coat?"

Hadley nodded. She would probably never have an opportunity like this again. To dissuade Wendell by his *own* choice without her ever having to tell him she had absolutely no interest in him and hurting his poor feelings. "We'll, um, need to walk," she reminded him, ignoring the little voice inside her head that mocked her for not admitting that the appeal here had nothing whatsoever to do with Wendell. "Are you *sure* you want—"

"Get your coat, Hadley."

She didn't wait around for Wood to come to his senses and change his mind. She went and got her coat.

And if she ran a brush through her hair and spritzed on a little perfume that Evie had given her for Christmas to compensate for the sexless bulky parka she donned, then only she had to know.

Wood was waiting by the front door in his leather jacket.

Her steps faltered. She might be warmer, but he wouldn't be. "You need a coat, too."

He shrugged, unconcerned. "I'll be fine."

"We could stop by Shane's and borrow one."

"And give the good sheriff a chance to talk you out of this?" Wood opened the door and nudged her through. "Don't think so."

He had a point. She snatched the black muffler from her own neck though, and held it out to him. "At least use this. If you end up catching pneumonia or something, I'd never forgive myself."

He took the long scarf and looped it around his neck. "Satisfied?"

"I would be if you had gloves, too."

He smiled and grabbed her hand, then tucked them both, her mitten and all, in his pocket. "This'll do."

She gulped a little, and concentrated hard on not falling down the steps beside him.

The night was clear, the dark sky studded with stars, easily visible despite the glow of the street-lights as they walked toward town. Hadley gathered herself enough to point out different places as they walked. "That's church row." She gestured to a tree-lined turnoff. "My dad's church—Lucius Commu-nity—and two others are on that street. It's really called Poplar Avenue, but with the town's only churches located there…" She shrugged. Even through her mitten she could feel the warmth of his long fingers wrapped around hers. The sensation was causing her to babble.

"Is there a hospital here?"

"A very small one. And we seem to have enough doctors and dentists to serve the town, fortunately. We even have a chiropractor." She eyed him. "Stu got laid up a while back after he tangled with an ornery cow. Up to then, he'd never been to a chiropractor in his life. Now he's a believer, though. I can give you his number if you're sore from the accident.''

"I'm surviving," he assured.

"But how does your forehead feel?"

His gaze slanted her way. "Like it tried to go through a windshield."

She bit her lip. "I'm so sorry."

His fingers squeezed hers a little. "Forget it."

But, of course, she couldn't. Their accident was the sole reason he was stuck in Lucius, and there was no point in pretending otherwise. Just because he'd chosen to pass the time helping her out of her situation with Wendell didn't change anything, other than to prove what a really nice man he was.

They passed the sheriff's office. The windows were dark. Shane was undoubtedly working on the house at the edge of town that he'd been building himself. In contrast, when they reached it, the Tipped Barrel was lit up like the Fourth of July. There was a spill of vehicles parked in front of the lively tavern. Her feet dragged to a halt, though, when she recognized one of them.

"What's wrong?"

Hadley wished she could pretend she hadn't seen her brother-in-law's truck. "My sister's husband is in there," she said after a moment.

"Judging by the number of cars, it looks like half the county is in there. Popular like you said."

"Yes." She tugged her hand out of the warm safety of his pocket. "The last time Charlie went to the Tipped Barrel, he got in a bar fight. My sister and he are still paying off the damages. He's not supposed to come here, at all.''

"Then call your brother. He's the sheriff."

Hadley started through the parking lot. "He is, and he'd probably have to lock Charlie up, and Charlie would lose his job, and Evie and my niece and nephews would be the ones to suffer the consequences. It'll have to be me. I'll just see you back at Tiff's.

He snorted, and caught her arm. "Whoa. Hold on. You think I'm going to let you go in there on your own? You've never been in a bar, remember? What was your brother-in-law fighting about?"

"Who knows? If he was drinking, and why else would he have gone there—" she pointed accusingly at the tavern "—other than to drink? Then he wouldn't need much reason. He's not really pleasant when he drinks.''

"And your sister stays with him because he's a great guy when he's not drinking?"

Hadley sighed. She stepped around a pile of slushy mud. "I really wish you'd go back to Tiff's."

"Why?"

She stopped. Flopped her hands to her sides. "Because this is embarrassing, okay? You're a nice guy, and there is probably nothing but trouble waiting inside that place. I'm not going to…to relax, and you're not going to meet anyone but Charlie, 'cause I can't let him stay in there! I think I've caused you enough problems. For heaven's sake, the last thing you should concern yourself with is my problems with my brothers and Wendell Pierce *or* Charlie Beckett.''

"How old are you?"

She faltered. "What? I'm twenty-seven. And no, you don't have to tell me how pathetic it is that I've never been into a bar at my age."

"Your concern for me is commendable but unnecessary," he said, his voice flat. "I've got ten years on you, sweetness, and a lifetime of managing my own way. If you're foolish enough to think I'll let you go in there to deal with your brother-in-law alone, then you're not as bright as I thought."

"I wish we'd never come out tonight," she muttered. "Well fine, Mr. In-Control, have it your way. But don't say I didn't warn you." She marched toward the entrance, not daring to think beyond getting through the front door.

Wood closed his hand over the back of her neck as they went inside. Instead of shivering from the contact, though, she found it comforting.

A couple Hadley had never seen before brushed against them as they hurried out the door, and Wood stepped even closer to her. She could feel the steadiness of him all down her spine, and it gave her enough courage to stop praying that Charlie wouldn't be inside after all and to start looking around for him.

There was a long, dark bar across the rear of the room. Smoke hung in the red-tinted air, and music blasted from the live group playing on a raised platform, not entirely disguising the clink of balls on the collection of pool tables or the voices from the people bellied up to the bar.

Wood lowered his head next to hers. "Do you see him?"

His cheek had brushed against hers, a hint of rasp in the contact. She shivered inside her coat. "No. I can't believe how many people are here."

"Friday night," Wood dismissed. "Maybe he's at one of the tables." Even as he spoke, he was moving forward. Hadley moved with him. They skirted the pool tables. Four in all, and all being used.

"What's he look like?" His cheek rasped against hers again.

How quickly her thoughts could scramble. She focused with an effort. The cigarette smoke was nearly choking her. "Shorter than you. Medium-brown hair. Kind of a husky build. I can't believe Charlie would come here again after—" She jumped when the smash of glass sounded nearby.

She'd barely had time to look in the direction of the fracas before she found herself firmly tucked behind Wood, his hand unrelentingly strong on hers as he held her there.

She peered around his wide shoulder to see three men scuffling near the bar, and sagged against Wood with relief. None of them were Charlie.

"Had? What the hell you doing here?"

She whirled around and nearly yanked her arm out of her socket thanks to Wood's grip. "Charlie." She tugged at Wood and he turned with her. "I could ask the same thing of you. Does Evie know you're here?"

Charlie made a face and lifted his drink. "What

makes you think she'd care? Your sister doesn't remember what the word fun even means.''

Hadley stepped closer to him, steeling herself against the stench of alcohol emanating from him. ''She's busy at home taking care of *your* children,'' she reminded, raising her voice over the noise, higher than she'd have liked. ''Come on. We'll drive you home.''

Charlie laughed at that, his bleary eyes looking from her to Wood. ''In what? Evie told me you'd busted up your truck again, along with someone else's. Nosy idiot, is what you are.''

''In your truck,'' she said tightly.

''Who says I wanna go home now, anyway?''

''What are you going to do when you do want to go? You're drunk. *You* can't drive.'' Frustration filled her. She reached out for him, but he pushed her back. His drink spilled over the front of her coat, and he stumbled.

Wood steadied her and caught Charlie up by the scruff of his neck in one fell swoop.

''Lemme go,'' he groused.

Wood ignored Charlie and looked at her. He still held her arm. ''You okay?''

She nodded, swiping at the liquid. Now this coat would need cleaning, too.

''Lemme go, I said! Who are you, anyway? Sure in hell couldn't be a friend of Had's. She's buttoned down tighter 'n a nun. Doesn't even know how to kiss a man, much less spread her legs—''

Wood grabbed Charlie's arm and leaned forward, speaking softly in the man's ear.

Charlie's mouth dropped. "Mind your own damned business." He shoved out at Wood, as if to hit him, but Wood easily sidestepped it, and Charlie tumbled forward, knocking into the table before him, scattering the occupants and sending glasses flying. He scrambled to his feet and launched himself at Wood.

Hadley cried out. "Stop it!"

But Wood did something fancy when he caught Charlie, halting the other man in his tracks.

He tried shrugging off Wood's grip and failed. "You pushed me!"

"I should have decked you," Wood said cuttingly, "instead of letting you fall on your face. You offended your sister-in-law. We're going now." He began marching Charlie toward the entrance, weaving around tables and customers without hesitation.

Hadley had a fleeting thought that Charlie would have been better off tangling with Shane's temper than Wood's. She eyed the people from the splintered table, offering a hurried apology as she watched Wood and her brother-in-law progress through the tavern. Wood's only hesitation was to stop and speak briefly to a blond cocktail waitress who was watching them all with a surprised expression. At the door, Wood looked back, clearly seeking out Hadley, and she hurried after them.

Outside, Charlie's attitude subsided considerably and he handed over his keys to Hadley without a quibble, making her wonder just what Wood had said to him. She half expected some comment from Wood when she got behind the wheel of the slightly bat-

tered SUV, but he didn't speak at all except to tell
Charlie to shut up when he started complaining about
Hadley driving his precious truck.

Lurching only slightly with the unfamiliar vehicle,
she drove out of the parking lot and headed toward
Evie and Charlie's home. When they arrived, Evie
came out of the small house, a blanket wrapped
tightly around her.

She took one look at Charlie and her expression
went tight. Then she glared at Hadley, as if it were
all her fault. "I'll have to get the truck from you
tomorrow," was all she said before she hustled her
husband inside and slammed the door shut.

Hadley sank back against the side of the SUV.
"Well. That went well. I should have just left Charlie
alone." She looked over at Wood. He was eyeing
the small house, no particular expression on his face
at all. "Why'd you have to go and make him mad
like that? He'll probably try to sue you or something." It'd be just like Charlie. Always trying to
make a quick buck that didn't involve an honest
day's work.

Wood spread his fingers, looking at his hand, as
if he were wishing he'd punched Charlie just as he'd
said. "He's put the moves on you before?"

She opened her mouth to deny it. "It was a long
time ago," she dismissed. He and Evie hadn't been
married too long. "And nothing happened, believe
me."

"How long ago?"

She glanced nervously at the brick house, but the
door was shut tight, the drapes drawn in the win-

dows. "I don't know. I was sixteen I think. I don't know why I even admitted it to you. Nobody else knows about it, so I'd appreciate you not saying anything to—"

"Did he hurt you?" His hand curled.

"Lord, no. And he didn't try again." It was humiliating even recalling the event. "Not that he'd want to. You heard him. He doesn't find me appealing at all, fortunately." She raked her fingers through her hair. "You know there's only one man in town who *does* find me appealing. And fighting that doesn't seem to do anything but cause problems. My accident with you. Going out together tonight." She pulled open the truck door and climbed in again.

After a moment Wood rounded the vehicle and got in, as well. She started the engine, but didn't put it into gear. She sighed after a moment. "Would you prefer to drive?"

"Yes. But I'll live with the disappointment."

She exhaled on a bewildered laugh at his dry assurance. "I don't understand you at all."

"Is your sister happy with him?"

Under any other circumstances, Hadley would have choked before she'd discuss family business with a stranger. But, even after such a short time, she couldn't view Wood Tolliver as a stranger.

If that made her foolish, so be it.

"I don't know," she answered truthfully. "She used to be. They were college sweethearts. But Evie doesn't share much these days. All I know is that she hasn't seemed happy about a lot of things for a while now." She shook her head. "Trying to talk to her hasn't done much good. She's always busy with the kids, or trying to fix something around that house, or telling me how I should be running Tiff's. I haven't seen her smile in a long time, and she has a beautiful smile. Her birthday is next week, and it just seems a sin that she'll be celebrating another year without that smile on her face. She isn't even having a party or anything. Says she's too tired and busy.''

''Throw one for her. Just lose Charlie's invitation.''

''If only.'' Hadley finally put the truck into gear. The vehicle rocked and jolted over the rutted drive before she turned onto the smoother, paved road. But Wood had a point. Maybe a surprise for Evie—one where she didn't have to do a single thing but sit back and enjoy—would be good for her. They could probably use the fellowship hall at her dad's church. Hadley would have to enlist Charlie's help in getting Evie there.

The parking lot outside of the Tipped Barrel was still clogged with cars when they passed. ''What did you tell the cocktail waitress when we were leaving?''

He looked a little surprised that she asked. ''How to reach me if Beckett doesn't pay any damages for tonight's episode.''

She gave him a quick look. ''Why?''

''I pushed him,'' was all he said.

She absorbed that as she drove the rest of the way through the quiet town. She made a U-turn on the street to park in front of Tiff's, and winced a little when one of the wheels bumped up over the curb and then back down again. So much for impressing the man.

The evening was officially a total bust.

She turned off the engine and climbed out, joining Wood on the sidewalk. He took her arm as they walked toward the house. Probably because he was afraid she'd fall on her face or something.

The front door was unlocked, as it always was, and she pushed it open. But Wood didn't release her arm right away when they entered, and she looked up at him. The porch lights behind him set off auburn glints in his hair. "Something wrong? Other than a genuinely unpleasant evening, I mean?"

He pushed the door shut until it latched softly. "Don't go back to the Tipped Barrel," he said. "The place is a complete dive." Then he lowered his head and pressed his mouth to hers.

She went stock-still. Shock, surprise, amazement. All three whisked through her with lightning speed. Then his hands—cool against her skin—cradled her face. Heat, want followed.

A soft sound rose in her throat and she leaned into him, nothing else existing but the feel of his lips softly caressing hers. "Wood—"

He broke the kiss with a soft oath. "For the record, Wendell Pierce *isn't* the only one to find you appealing." Then he stepped back from her. "Good night, Hadley."

Thank heavens for the wall behind her. It held her up. "Good night, Wood."

But he probably hadn't heard her shaking response. He'd already disappeared down the hallway.

Chapter Five

"Heard there was something of a ruckus last night at the Tipped Barrel."

Dane looked up from the bumper he was removing from the Shelby. Shane Golightly stood in the sunlight streaming through the open bay of Stu's garage. "So?"

Shane's jaw cocked to one side. He looked over his shoulder to where Stu had his head under the hood of Hadley's pickup, then walked closer, ostensibly studying the Shelby up on the rack. "Why are you still in Lucius?"

Dane pulled off the safety goggles Stu had loaned him, letting them hang loose around his neck. "You treat all visitors to such a welcome? No wonder this town is no bigger than my thumb. Chamber of Commerce must love you.'' He jerked his head toward the window between the office and the service bays. ''Your sister is in there, talking to Riva.''

''Stay away from her.''

''I've never been one to follow other people's orders.''

''Why am I not surprised?'' Shane kept his voice low. ''It may suit me, for the moment, not to run you out of town, but don't expect that to last. Hadley doesn't need someone like you messing in her life.''

''Maybe she doesn't need her brothers messing in her life, either. Ever thought your attention might be better focused on Evie?'' As far as Dane was concerned, it was the blond-haired sister who needed some intervention in her life, not the thoroughly engaging Hadley.

''What's that supposed to mean?''

Dane donned the goggles again and picked up the crowbar. ''Ask Hadley. I'm just a guy trying to get his car fixed.'' He knew Evie had retrieved the SUV early that morning, because he'd overheard the sharp words the woman exchanged with her sister and had barely contained his urge to interrupt them and defend Hadley since Hadley didn't seem to do much of it on her own.

The sheriff snorted. ''Yeah, and I wear a pink tutu on Friday afternoons.''

''Whatever floats your boat, Sheriff.'' Dane attacked the mangled bumper again.

Shane leaned in a little closer. ''Just a warning here, *Tolliver*. You're hiding something and we both know it. If you hurt my sister, you'll regret it, I promise you." Then he straightened and headed around the car toward the cramped office.

Dane finally found purchase with the crowbar, and the bumper peeled away with a screech. He dropped the crowbar and caught the ruined bumper and dumped it to one side.

The god-awful racket he created felt curiously satisfying.

He pulled off the work gloves and goggles and left them on the workbench. He lifted a hand in a wave to Hadley, who was watching him through the office window, and told Stu he'd check back later on the car's progress.

Stu nodded. He'd already agreed to get Hadley's truck fixed before putting his attention to the Shelby with the provision that Wood loan some of his elbow grease to the autobody repairs. Lord knew Stu didn't want him having any reason to be in Lucius a minute longer than necessary.

With the Golightlys seemingly occupied, Dane returned to his room at Tiff's where he spent a few solid hours on the phone with his assistant, Laura. It didn't matter that it was a Saturday. Most weeks they worked seven days straight. What was inconvenient, though, was dealing with business without aid of a fax or computer or anything other than his cell phone and his own notes spread across the foot of the bed. But they managed to keep the necessities under control. And dictating letters was pretty much the same regardless of the setting.

"Oh. One more thing." He told her about his conversation with Mandy Manning at the Tipped Barrel.

"Be sure and wire her the funds today to cover the damages," he said when she finally started winding down. "And don't send enough that someone accuses anyone of bribery," he muttered. A soft knock on his bedroom door interrupted the annoyingly fresh memory of Shane Golightly's accusation of bribery. He ended his call and pulled open the door.

Hadley stood on the other side, her arms filled with linens. "Hi."

He'd done no more than wave hello and goodbye at Stu's garage, and had deliberately gone to the Luscious Lucius for breakfast in order to avoid her.

Not exactly chivalrous behavior, nor adult. But kissing her the night before hadn't been the smartest thing he'd ever done, either. One of the most pleasurable? Yes. Smart? No.

"What's all that?" He gestured to her burden.

"Emergency candles and clean linens. And an extra blanket for your bed. The temperature's supposed to drop again in the next day or two." She didn't quite meet his eyes as she looked past him into the room. "If it's not an inconvenient time, I'll get you all set up."

He knew there was no way she could see the contents of his notes spread on the bed from where she stood, or the engraved Rutherford Industries logo topping them. But he didn't intend to chance a closer look from her, either.

"I won't get cold." Particularly not now, knowing that her lips tasted sweeter than they looked. Or knowing that she slept as close as the other side of a wall. That when she'd risen that morning, he'd listened to the sound of water running in the old-fashioned bathroom tucked between them and had cursed his imagination that had never before plagued him with such painful vividness.

"Are you sure? It's no trouble. And I know how many blankets are on your bed, Wood. Same as were on everyone else's."

"Yours?" He was a glutton for punishment.

She blinked. "Well, yes. And truly, the weather forecasters are all saying the temperature—"

"Fine. Give me the stuff." He reached for the blanket and she tried handing it to him, but the entire bundle in her arms fell in the process. Fat white candles rolled across the hall and yellow terry cloth towels, white sheets, and soft blue wool surrounded her, an ocean of color. "Sorry." He knelt and she knelt and their heads knocked.

He cursed, feeling the slight impact against his injured forehead with the force of a sledgehammer.

"Oh, Lord." Her hands caught at his shoulders. "I can't believe I did that. Sit down."

He didn't have much choice with her tugging at him the way she was. He sat down, leaning his head back against the doorjamb. He'd never really seen stars before, but when he closed his eyes, pricks of light sparked behind his eyelids.

He was vaguely aware of Hadley stepping over him, dislodging the jumble of linens. He heard water running and then she returned.

"I'm going to take off the bandage, okay?" Her fingers were cool and gentle on his face as she peeled it away, then she sucked in her breath. "Oh, Wood.

This cut looks terrible. Come on. I'm taking you to the hospital, right now. We should have done it right after the accident, no matter what you wanted.''

She pressed the wet, cold washcloth to his forehead, then tucked her hands under his arms, as if she fully intended to lift him up if he didn't cooperate.

''I've had worse cuts.'' And he hadn't seen stars then because he'd generally been out cold after the fact. He stopped her efforts by closing his hands around her slender waist. ''Stop.'' He pulled her down, and her slight weight settled over his thighs. It went some way to alleviating the throbbing in his head, since his blood immediately headed south. He kept her in place with one arm and held the cloth to his head with the other.

Nirvana.

''Worse cuts from what?'' Her voice was breathy. Soft.

He opened his eyes a slit and looked at her. ''From a long time ago,'' he admitted. ''Racing days.''

She sucked in the corner of her lip for an infinitesimal moment that nevertheless felt indelibly etched in time. ''Horse racing? Foot racing? Car racing?''

''Car.'' NASCAR, to be exact. And one of the happiest times in his life. Time that had been too short because other responsibilities had taken priority. Responsibilities that grew with each passing year.

She lifted her hand, only to curl her fingers tightly together and drop it to her lap again. ''Were you hurt very badly?''

He closed his eyes again, imagining her fingers touching him. "Nothin' I couldn't recover from," he drawled.

"That's how you got these?"

He went still when imagination became reality and her fingertips gently grazed over the scars near his eye. "Yeah."

"I'd be too afraid to race a car." Her voice was whisper soft.

He smiled. "Sweetness, you could race. You'd just have a hard time finding drivers to get on the same track with you."

Her touch fell away. "I'm really bad."

He opened his eyes. "You could be better," he said honestly.

To her credit, she didn't take offense. "Maybe you could teach me. Give me some pointers. Not for free or anything," she added hastily. "I'd be willing to pay you."

"I don't want your money, Hadley." He was starting to want something far more personal than that, which was so far out of the question he felt lower than pond scum even thinking it.

It wasn't a sensation he was used to experiencing.

"Right." She shifted, but his arm still anchored her in place. She started folding a towel across her splayed legs, her movements jerky enough that he knew she was not entirely comfortable sitting there on the floor in the hallway the way they were. "You just want to be on your way as soon as possible," she said. "I understand, believe me."

He didn't deny it, and knew she'd assume she was correct. "You've wanted to leave Lucius yourself?"

"I did leave for a while. For college. Then my mom got sick so I came back home."

And stayed to run Tiff's. His palm spread over the small of her back. God, she was so slender. Yet she didn't feel made of bones and snobbery the way his usual women did.

Hadley's not usual, and she's not your woman.

He mentally kicked the conscientious whisper in the teeth. "What'd you study?"

"Hmm? Oh. Business courses."

"Dull." He oughta know. Business for him hadn't been interesting since he'd left behind the company he and Wood had formed to take on the mantle of Rutherford Industries.

She laughed a little and reached for another towel. Her soft breast brushed against his chest, feeling fuller than he'd have expected giving her habitually too-large clothing. "Dull is right. You probably studied something very exciting."

The pain in his head had subsided to a muted throb. "What makes you think that?"

"Well, you just said you were a race car driver, right? You don't seem the kind of man who would be satisfied putting on a tie every morning and going to some stuffy nine-to-five."

"I do wear a tie most days," he assured dryly. Hell, Darby had called him the king of Armani. And he couldn't remember the last time, if ever, his business day had been concluded by five o'clock.

"What is it that you do?"

"I own a business."

"In Indiana?"

"Yes." It wasn't entirely a lie. RTM was based there.

"Do you like it?"

"I'm good at it," he said after a moment. "Liking it doesn't have much to do with that."

"Rather be racing?"

"Racing. Building cars. Fixing cars." Exactly what he and Wood had planned so long ago.

"Hmm." Her fingers plucked at the tidy stack of towels that had been growing on her lap, and her cheeks looked rosy. "Are you married?"

"Do I *act* married?" Irritation skittered down his spine.

"That's not exactly an answer."

"I kissed you, remember?" Had he read her so wrong, then? Was that moment of insanity only memorable for him?

"And you stopped." Her cheeks were even redder, but her soft mouth was set. Resolute.

"Would you have preferred I continue?" He slid his palm up her spine. Threaded his fingers through her abundantly silky hair and cupped the back of her warm, slender neck. "Believe me, sweetness, it would've been no hardship."

"You were just being nice. Kind. Because of what Charlie said and all."

"I'm *not* nice, or kind," he said evenly. *Nice* hadn't gotten Rutherford Industries to where it was today. *Kind* hadn't been the words used by the companies he'd taken over. And *nice* sure in hell wouldn't involve lying about his reason for remaining in Lucius. "I'm manipulative and controlling and I get what I want."

The power of being a Rutherford. The name was pretty much synonymous with American royalty.

She looked skeptical. "It's not a sin to be kind, you know."

"It is in my father's world. There's no time for kindness there." Only the business. Always the business. Whether he liked it or not.

Her lashes dipped. She nibbled her lip with the slightest edge of her pearly, white teeth. "I think that's sad," she said after a moment.

Dane didn't want sympathy. He wanted payback. Pure and simple. And nice, kind men didn't use perfectly innocent young women to achieve it.

Then her lashes lifted and her gaze found his. "Well? Are you married or not?"

He'd borrowed Wood Tolliver's identity. He could easily have borrowed Wood's wife, at least in name. It would solve one thing, at least. Hadley Golightly wasn't likely to give him a second glance if she believed he had a wife somewhere. She'd do her level best to make up for the inconvenience of their accident, and she'd be hospitable while she was about it, but that would be all. He knew it in his bones. He could easily remove her from his own temptation, just by telling her one simple three-letter word.

Yes.

"No," he said. "I've never been married."

Her expression didn't change, but her eyes softened. She covered his hand, gently pressing against it, directing the damp washcloth more carefully against his cut. "That's…good," she finally whispered.

Oh, yeah. It was good all right. He felt her body against his from chest to thigh and felt as randy as a teenager as a result.

"What's going on here?"

Hadley nearly jumped out of her skin at the tight voice. The stack of towels she'd refolded tumbled right off her legs and she scrambled from Wood's lap, looking up at Shane and feeling as guilty as if she'd been caught running naked down Main Street.

Wood closed his hand over hers, preventing her from going far. "Your sister's been rendering first aid," he said smoothly.

Hadley's face felt on fire. Her entire body felt flushed, for that matter, and not all of it stemmed from embarrassment at her big brother catching them.

"Mebbe you need to go to the hospital. I'll drive you on over." It wasn't a suggestion, but a decree.

Wood pushed to his feet, bringing her with him. "Sorry to disappoint you, Sheriff. I'm pretty comfortable right here."

Hadley looked from Wood to her brother. He hardly showed it, but she knew Shane was furious and for some reason Wood was egging him on. "Shane, what are you doing here?"

He eyed her. "You wanted me to split more logs for you before tonight, remember?"

Of course. She felt even more idiotic. Shane always went out of his way to make sure she had plenty of wood on hand in case the power went out, something the old house often suffered during a storm, and she'd specifically asked him to help her, given the current weather forecast.

"Mr. Tolliver can help me," Shane went on.

She made a face. "Now you're just being ridiculous. If anything, Wood should be resting. I nearly boxed Stu's ears for letting him work at the garage this morning on that poor car of his." She crouched down and swept up the linens in one huge armload and dropped the candles on top. "And I have work to do, if you don't mind."

She shouldered past Wood into his room. She dumped the blanket and fresh sheets on the head of the bed and rapidly folded the clean towels, yet again, to leave in a stack on the dresser near the bathroom door. She set out the candles, checked that there were still plenty of matches in the antique silver box of them on the dresser and then turned back to the bed, only to find Wood was already scooping up his paperwork that was scattered over the foot of it.

Aware of her brother still standing near the doorway watching with plain displeasure, she whipped off the green-and-yellow quilt. In minutes, she'd stripped and remade the bed with clean linens and the extra blanket. Then she smoothed the quilt top back in place, plumped the pillows a little and hurried to the door, the old sheets in her arms. "Sorry for interrupting your work," she murmured to Wood, nodding at the sheaf clenched in his long fingers.

She sailed past her brother and dumped the sheets down the laundry chute hidden behind a panel in the hallway. They'd land smack dab in the center of the laundry room in the basement. When Shane didn't move, she turned and glared at him. "I can call Dad about the logs if you prefer. He's forever offering to help."

"I said I'd do it," Shane groused. His boots scraped along the fussy carpet runner as he stomped past her, then out the back way through the kitchen. If the slam of that door was anything to go by, Hadley knew his temper was in fine form.

She let out a long breath and cast a sideways look at Wood. "He's not usually so disagreeable."

"You don't have to make excuses for anyone, Hadley."

Maybe she didn't. But he was certainly the first person to tell her so. She didn't know what it was about the man that alternately made her feel strong and brave, then...not.

So she fell back on the safe and familiar.

"I'll have lunch out within the hour. Sorry to have disturbed you." She turned to go. She needed to change the linens in the tower room also, and leave out extra blankets for all the regulars, who took care of their own laundry. But she stopped. "Are you sure your head is all right?" She looked at him.

His expression seemed stark.

"Save your worry, Hadley, for someone who needs it."

Something curled inside her at the words. Not a command or a rebuff.

But a plea?

She dismissed the very notion of it. Her imagination had clearly shifted into overdrive.

She nodded and went to finish her tasks and when she set out lunch that day, she resumed her usual custom of spending the peaceful hour in her room with her papers and pen. But instead of furiously scribbling out the stories that were forever tumbling around inside her head, she sat on her cushioned window seat and stared blindly out the window, the pen seemingly forgotten in her hand.

The only character in her thoughts was a real, live person named Wood Tolliver.

The weather forecast proved correct and a fresh snowstorm hit that evening after dinner. Vince kept the fire stoked with the additional split logs Shane had left. Hadley mixed up a large pot of hot cocoa, and most everyone congregated in the parlor where the fire cheerfully blazed despite the howling wind that rattled the windows.

Everyone except Wood.

When she'd finished up the phone calls of arrangements for Evie's surprise birthday party, Hadley tried not to let his absence concern her. But it was a hopeless endeavor, doomed to failure from the very start. And finally, while everyone else was occupied with a raucous game of charades, she set aside her party notes and went to the kitchen. She fixed a tray of cocoa and cookies and carried it down the hall. She rapped her knuckles softly against the door panel.

He didn't answer, and standing in the hall far longer than necessary only ended up making her feel particularly pathetic. The man was finally getting some well-deserved rest.

Who could blame him for that?

She returned the tray to the kitchen and bade a good-night to everyone in the parlor. She noticed that Nikki Day was no longer there. Mrs. Ardelle told her that she'd retired. Apparently during Hadley's futile wait outside Wood's door.

As far as Hadley had been able to determine, Nikki—while friendly and polite—didn't seem to be having a particularly enjoyable time. She was clearly pregnant, but had only picked at her dinner. And Mrs. Ardelle had said she'd done the same during lunch.

If only to ease her concern about *someone,* Hadley went up the tower and knocked softly on that door.

After a moment it opened. Nikki's face looked pale and drawn. "Yes?"

"I just wanted to make certain you were warm enough up here. If you're not, I could start a fire in the fireplace for you."

Nikki pushed up the sleeves of her dark-green sweater. "I'm fine without it. And the room is lovely." She looked away for a moment.

Hadley had to curtail the impulse to give the woman a hug. She looked as if she needed one just as badly as Joanie ever had. But she also recognized the woman's innate sense of privacy and didn't want to cause her any discomfort. "If the storm doesn't deliver too much snow, you'll be all set for the sleigh ride you requested. Tomorrow after lunch."

A shadow came and went in the other woman's

eyes. "You must think it very odd that I've come here this way. Going on things like sleigh rides alone."

"I think you have your reasons," Hadley said honestly. "And it's a pleasure for me to make your stay special in the same way my mother must have for your relatives who were here before."

"My fiancé's parents, actually," Nikki said. "They were here on their honeymoon. Cody always talked about us coming here." She pressed her lips together for a moment. "I never thought I'd be coming by myself."

Forget privacy. Hadley reached out and gently squeezed Nikki's cool hands. "If there's anything I can do, you just ask. I have all of the guest registers that my mother used. Maybe you'd like to look at them sometime. I'm sure we'd find their visit listed."

Nikki's eyes looked moist. She nodded. "Thank you." She squeezed Hadley's hands in return, then reached for the door. "Good night."

"Good night." Hadley headed back downstairs and went to her room. It was chilly and she added a blanket to her own bed the way she had the others, then—since there was no sound at all through the door to Wood's room—she indulged herself with a hot bath and a book. No matter the fact that she'd retired for the night, her mind was simply too busy to sleep.

The book was good, and the bathwater was cold, the bubbles long gone when the lights flickered and went out.

She stared into the inky darkness. Well, great. But

it wasn't the first time she'd dealt with a power outage, and as long as she ran Tiff's, it would undoubtedly not be the last.

She tossed aside her book, well out of the way of any water splashing, and climbed out of the tub, racing the towel over her chilled skin and fumbling into her robe again. Going by feel, she pulled the stopper in the tub and padded into her bedroom. She lit the oil lamp on her dresser and went back into the bathroom, tidying up by the dim light there. Then she went out into the hallway and checked the rest of the house.

All was still. Silent, save the slow tick of the wind-up anniversary clock sitting on the mantel in the parlor.

She pulled back the lacy curtains to look out the front.

The entire street was dark, meaning it wasn't just Tiff's that suffered a power outage this time. By the moonlight, however, she could see the fresh drifts of snow in the street.

It took her a moment to make a shape out of the shadows. But she realized when the shadow moved, becoming two distinct forms in the middle of the street where the snowfall wasn't quite as deep, that it was two people.

One headed off down the street, a genderless blob of dark coat and hat. One headed toward Tiff's.

She straightened abruptly, letting the curtain fall back into place. She had no time to escape down the hall to her room, and in seconds, she heard footsteps on the porch, followed by the creak of the front door.

Great. Just great.

She didn't even have the sense to extinguish her oil lamp. She just stood there in the parlor, listening. Visualizing his motions, along with his sounds—closing the door behind him, the creak of his leather jacket being removed, the nearly soundless tread up the hallway, passing the parlor doorway.

Pausing.

"So you're the glow in an otherwise dark night."

She nearly jumped out of her skin. The lamp bobbled in her hand, and she quickly steadied it before she dropped the infernal thing and set fire to the place. Her other hand clutched the lapels of her robe together. "The power is out."

He was kind enough not to point out that he'd undoubtedly noticed that particular point. "Is everything okay?"

She wanted to ask him about the person he'd been with. An assignation? She'd never before used that word. Never had cause. She didn't have *cause* now. The man was only a guest—a reluctant visitor in Lucius—a situation for which she was responsible. "Everything is fine. I was just, um, checking the place over. To be safe." It was the gospel truth, yet she still felt as if she'd been caught spying on him. She hurriedly left the parlor. "Here." She extended the lamp to him. "You'll need this to get around."

"It's late."

So, *he* could state the obvious as well as she could. "Yes." And maybe that was why she felt unaccountably emotional. "Do you want the lamp or not? I can find my way around here with my eyes closed."

He still didn't take it. He took another step, entering further into her small circle of light. She could see her black scarf hanging from one hand, his jacket from the other.

"You're upset."

"Of course I'm not. I have nothing to be upset about."

Another step. His head tilted a little to one side. "Hadley, it's just a power outage. Nothing to worry about."

If only she'd been quick enough to use that as an excuse. "Right. I know." Did she smell perfume on him? "Well, here. Take the lamp. Don't want you tripping on something and cracking open your head more than it's already been."

"I don't need the lamp." He tossed aside the jacket and scarf and closed his hands over her forearms beneath the wide sleeves of her robe. "I want to know what's got you so jumpy. Is it your brother-in-law again?"

"What? No. Charlie never bothers me. Last night was just because, because he was drunk." His fingers were cold, yet they still made her skin heat, particularly when his hands slid farther up, curving around her elbows. "I told you that."

His thumbs glided over her skin. "Then, what's wrong, Hadley?"

Each gentle brush of his thumbs yanked her nerves tighter. The lamp's flame danced inside the tall glass globe, and she tightened her shaking grip on it, holding it sternly between them. But keeping control of one part of her left her tongue unfortunately unguarded.

''Who was that woman? I thought you didn't know anyone in Lucius.''

Chapter Six

Dane cursed himself. He had no desire to upset Hadley. "I went to the Tipped Barrel." Which didn't answer her question at all.

Her eyes looked liquid in the flickering light. "You probably shouldn't drink with a head injury."

He forced himself to keep his touch light on her arms, though his fingers didn't want much more in life at the moment than to keep exploring. To see if her skin was as exquisitely soft everywhere else. "I wasn't. I played some pool." And got Mandy's latest report on the investigation.

She looked disbelieving. "Oh. Well. Hope you didn't lose your shirt or anything. Vince plays pool there sometimes. And Palmer Frame. He was one of the EMTs who came with the ambulance."

"Yeah. I saw him there. He mentioned the surprise party you're throwing for your sister. Sounds like you've invited half the town. I didn't see Charlie."

"Well, that's something at least," she murmured. She lightened up her guarded hold of the lamp, moving one hand to clutch the overlapping lapels of her pale robe tightly together. As if he needed any more reasons to wonder what she wore beneath it.

The thick terry cloth covered her from head to toe, and the only breach in it—which he'd already taken advantage of—seemed to be the wide sleeves. He needed her to go to bed so he could stop letting himself be distracted by her.

"The place was pretty quiet, actually. Probably because of the storm."

She nodded. Pressed her lips together and nodded again. "Well."

Yeah. Well. He let go of her and grabbed up his jacket from the back of the chair where it had landed. "Lead the way," he said. "I'll follow."

She moved past him, and he got a heady hint of some warm, feminine scent. Flowery, but not sweet. And her hair was damp at the ends, he realized as she walked down the hall, turning back now and again as if he were likely to get lost along the way. Shower or bathtub, he wondered, and kicked himself for it, since he was the one to suffer the consequences of wondering.

She paused near his door until he'd opened it, then followed him inside when he did. He went stock-still for a moment, but she didn't look at him as she crossed to the dresser and set the lamp on it long enough to light the two fat candles she'd left there earlier that day. Then she slipped out of his bedroom again.

"Good night, Wood." In a half-dozen steps, she disappeared behind her own bedroom door, giving him no hint whatsoever of the room beyond her door.

Probably pure innocence, to suit its occupant.

He closed his own door and curtailed the impulse to thump his head against the wood in frustration. The candlelight flickered over the walls, casting enough light for him to see by. He dumped the jacket on the end of the bed, grabbed one of the candles and went into the adjoining bathroom.

The delicate sent of flowers hit him with the subtle finesse of a two-by-four. He shoved the candle on the glass shelf above the sink and sat on the edge of the old-fashioned, deep tub. He knew if he reached down and touched the bottom, it would still be wet.

His mind filled with the image of Hadley in the tub and he deliberately eyed his dim reflection in the mirror across from him to banish the thoughts. He was losing it, pure and simple.

He didn't like it.

He yanked off his shirt and went to the sink, flipping on the faucet to douse his face with the frigid water.

It seeped beneath the bandage on his forehead, setting off a fresh new pain, and it didn't do squat to cool anything else. Swearing under his breath, he returned to the bedroom.

There wasn't even room to pace, and for a minute he wished he'd never started this damn quest. That he was still in Kentucky. He had plenty of space to pace there.

In his office at Rutherford Industries.

In his spacious, empty apartment where the only scent left behind by any woman was the expensive one his mother wore on her very rare visits.

The women Dane knew didn't smell of a field of wildflowers in the middle of the bloody damn winter. They wore designer clothes and designer scents and lingerie created with the sole intent of sophisticated seduction. They knew how to use others just as much as he did, he never invited them into his personal space, and he never had to worry that he'd hurt a single one of them.

He wasn't into hurting innocents.

So he needed to get his head back in the game. He needed to find his control again. He needed to find Alan Michaels, since the police were clearly incapable of it, and make him finally pay for what he'd done all those years ago.

Maybe some would consider being institutionalized punishment enough for kidnapping Dane's little sister, but Dane didn't. Darby had only been nine. And even though she'd been recovered, the effects of that time had torn apart their family. Michaels should have been rotting in jail because of it, not strolling the green lawns and calming corridors of an institution too sensitive and lax to even keep hold of one of their more notorious ''guests.''

Michaels *would* pay, and once he had, Dane's life would be on course again.

All he needed to do was keep himself focused.

* * *

"I think the focus is off." Hadley peered through the binoculars that Wendell had stuck in her face. He'd shown up at church that morning, scooting into the pew beside her, and she hadn't shaken him since. Not during church. Not after church when he'd insisted on driving her back to Tiff's. And certainly not since then, because he'd pulled the binoculars out of his glove box and trooped after her into Tiff's, despite her warnings that she needed to get lunch on for her guests.

She started to adjust the binoculars again, but Wendell clucked and whipped the glasses out of her hand and looked through them himself.

"No, I think it's perfect," he assured. His dress boots crunched in the snow as he stepped behind her. He lowered the binoculars back to her face, his arms circling her from behind. "Now look again."

Hadley didn't *want* to look, and she didn't want Wendell having his arms virtually surrounding her. But there the heavy black binoculars were, two inches from her nose, held firmly in place by Wendell's knobby fingers.

Which made her feel unkind, so she leaned forward, stifling a sigh. All she saw through them was a reflection of her own eyelashes and a blur of tree branches.

"Well? It's a perfect view of the cardinal, Had."

She closed her eyes for a moment, crossed her fingers inside her mittens. "A perfect view," she agreed. Then she ducked underneath his circling arms and faced him. She'd tolerated him all morning, and she had things she needed to do. Important things. Like rearranging the soup cans in the cupboard.

She felt unkind all over again. "So, Stu happened to tell you how much I enjoy bird-watching?"

"Just yesterday." Wendell lifted the binoculars to his nose and peered intently at the trees in the distance. His smile was so wide it nearly reached around his head. "I never thought I'd find a woman who'd fit so well into my life, Had. I knew we were well suited. When we're married, we'll be as comfortable as old socks."

She tugged on her ear. Hugged her arms closer, though the sun was climbing bright and warm against the cold day. "Wendell, I haven't agreed to marry you." Much less date the man.

He waved a hand though the binoculars stayed glued to his narrow face. "Oh, I know, dear. Take all the time you need."

His tone was clear that he considered her capitulation a foregone conclusion. "I don't really like old socks, Wendell."

"Did you say something, dear?"

She shook her head. If he called her *dear* one more time, she might run screaming all the way to the state line. "I have to get lunch finished, Wendell." She hoped to heaven he didn't take that as an invitation.

"Hmm." He continued watching his beloved cardinals. She figured when she wasn't standing there holding him back, he'd probably traipse considerably closer to the woods to get a better look.

She stomped the snow from her boots and went

up the back steps and in through the kitchen, tossing her good wool coat on the hook and not much caring when she missed. "I'm going to strangle him," she muttered under her breath as she went to the stove and gave the homemade chicken soup a vicious stir. "Maybe whip him a time or two."

No wonder Stu hadn't shown his face at church that morning. He probably *wasn't* working at the garage as she'd heard from Wendell. More likely, he was just hiding out from her, knowing she'd be furious when she learned what he'd told Wendell.

"Attack him with that deadly wooden spoon you're wielding. Ought to be punishment enough for whatever he's done."

She whirled around. Chunks of celery and carrot flew off her spoon and hit the counter with a splat. "Wood. I didn't see you."

He lifted the newspaper in his hand. "Just walked in to get some coffee. Who are you plotting against?"

She wished she didn't recall so vividly what his fingers felt like stroking the tender skin on the inside of her elbows. "Stu. He sicced Wendell on me again." She wiped up the spill and rinsed the spoon at the sink. "Telling him I like bird-watching. It's just mean, that's all. Wendell *loves* bird-watching and frankly, well, frankly I couldn't care less!" She craned her neck, peering out the window over the sink. "He's out there right now, imagining us rocking away on the front porch, twin binoculars in hand."

"Thought women liked to hear it when a man wanted to grow old with her."

"Ha! I'm not talking about future years, Wood. That'd be us right now if he had the chance. He's convinced we're suited like two 'old socks' for goodness' sake, and it's all my brothers' fault!'' She wiped her hands and yanked the towel into a neat fold over the oven handle. "Old socks. *No* thank you."

"Probably would do better to tell Wendell and your brothers that," Wood murmured.

"I have! I've told them *all* that. But does it matter? Heck no. They just keep telling good little Hadley what to do, making her decisions for her, choosing her paths—" She cut off the mindless rant. Drew in a deep breath. Let it out slowly. Focused on Wood. "Coffee," she remembered, and reached for the mug and the pot. She hadn't seen him earlier that day, and she'd told herself that she hadn't missed him.

Of course, she'd had to ask forgiveness during the silent prayers in church for that particular lie.

"Here." She already knew he took it black, so didn't offer milk or sugar when she handed it to him. "Wendell's going to come in here any minute, call me 'dear,' and go through the rest of the day, secure in his mind that one day, he'll have his old-sock wife handily nearby. And why wouldn't he? It's not as if he's ever seen me with another man." So much for stopping the rant. "There are hardly *any* single men around here and of the decent ones, two are already my brothers and right now, I'm not feeling so kindly toward either one that I'm still certain *they're* decent! Don't suppose you'd kiss me again or something right here in God's broad daylight so he could see, would you?''

She didn't dare look at him, so embarrassed was she at her own plea. ''I know I have no right to ask any favors of you, but I swear, Wood, they're going to marry me off to him.'' She pressed her hand to her chest. ''And that'll be my life. I'll be organized right into it, just like I was organized into running Tiff's.''

''Sit down.'' His hands closed over her shoulders and she found herself being nudged inexorably toward one of the iron chairs around the small table in the sunny bay of windows. ''This place was your mother's, wasn't it? I thought you wanted to run it.''

She curled her fingers into her fists until she could feel the pricks of her nails. He crouched down in front of her, his hands resting lightly on the seat on either side of her knees. And she ought to have felt hemmed in, just the way she'd felt by Wendell, but she didn't.

''I didn't mean that.'' How could she? Tiff's had been her mother's dream. Tiff's and marriage to Beau Golightly, who'd been the only father Hadley had ever known. ''I'm just... I don't know what I'm saying. See? I'm so frustrated. Would you—'' she swallowed ''—be willing to try the Tipped Barrel again? I know it wasn't much of a success the other night, and you wouldn't have to really, you know, act interested in me or...or anything.'' She was humiliating herself right and left. ''You could play pool like you did last night, then the evening wouldn't be a complete bore!''

He exhaled. "Nothing about you is boring, Hadley."

She laughed, wanting to cry. "Everything about me is boring," she whispered fiercely, "and that's why Wendell thinks we're so *perfect* for each other!" And she'd just asked this man to kiss her, this man who'd been nothing but nice to her, who clearly had some other interest already given the woman—and she was sure it *had* been a woman—he'd met the night before.

And the most embarrassing part of it all was that she wasn't sure asking him to kiss her had anything really to do with Wendell at all.

"First," he said gruffly, "you need to stay out of the Tipped Barrel. I shouldn't have taken you in there in the first place. It's a dive. And secondly, stop worrying. You can't be forced into marrying someone."

She pushed his hands away and rose, yanking down the hem of the beige cable-knit sweater she wore over a long beige skirt. "Easy for you to say. You've probably never done anything in your entire life that you didn't choose to do."

His lips twisted as he rose. "Then you'd be wrong, sweetness, believe me."

When nothing else seemed fit to stop her runaway rant, his flat voice did the job. And she could tell by his expression that asking him what he was referring to would get her nowhere. She exhaled. Switched subjects. "How does your head feel today?"

"Like the drum corps beating inside it have finally taken a breather." He lifted his hand. "And don't start in with the apologies again."

He didn't have knobby fingers. They were long, blunt tipped and capable looking. Capable of wielding tools, steering wheels and willing women.

She swallowed and turned back to the stove once more. "I'm glad you're feeling a little better," she managed evenly. "Will you be staying in for lunch?"

The back door opened without ceremony, and Wendell trooped in, his binoculars hanging from the long strap around his lanky neck. His orange-and-blue-plaid scarf straggled around his serviceable parka, and Hadley felt her nerves tighten up even more when he didn't so much as lift an eyebrow at Wood's presence in the kitchen.

Why would he? After all, Hadley ran a boardinghouse. There were plenty of people who were often around. Just because Wood was six-plus feet of palpitation-inspiring masculinity, it didn't mean diddly to Wendell.

Wendell rounded the counter and bussed Hadley's cheek. "See you later, dear."

Her molars ground together and she just stood there, mute, as he bounded through Tiff's. Even when she heard the front door slam shut, she didn't move, because if she did, she very much feared she was going to scream her head off.

"Hadley?"

She closed her eyes for a moment. Prayed for sanity. She wasn't going to be anyone's *old sock.* She just wasn't. "Yes, Wood?"

"Your soup is boiling over."

She jerked. Looked. "Oh, rats, bats and spiders,"

she muttered as she hurriedly turned off the flame under the pot. The stovetop was a mess. She yanked the pot off and stuck it in the sink, cleaned up the stove, then ladled the soup into the tureen that she'd already set out.

When it was full, she started to lift it, but Wood nudged her hands away. "I'll get it," he murmured.

Kindness. More kindnesses. Instead of warming her, it made her want to throw something.

She gathered up the rest of the lunch items and carried them out to the dining room. Arranged it mindlessly, rang the bell and grabbed her coat again.

She went out the back door, stomped around the side of the house, and headed up the street. By the time she made it to Stu's garage, her temper—rather than being walked out—had only increased.

Her truck was sitting in the lot, hood closed, and she was headed for the office when she saw Evie's trio of kids playing on the snow drifting up the side of the building.

Her irritation with Stu took a hiatus and she headed over to the kids. She hadn't seen them at church that morning, either. Not that their absence was particularly unusual. Charlie—to Beau's dismay—wasn't a very church-going man. "Hey, guys. What's up? How's the arm?"

Alan, the eldest at ten, shrugged. He'd broken his arm before Christmas playing football with some bigger kids. "It itches."

She nodded sympathetically. Julie and Trev, eight and six respectively, were using a plastic cup to dig holes in the snow. "Your mom inside?"

"Yeah." Alan leaned against the wall and kicked his foot desultorily back against it. "She wants Uncle Stu to watch us while she goes to Billings."

"I wanna go to Billings," Julie complained.

"I wanna go to Auntie Had's," Trevor said. He smiled his winsome smile up at Hadley. He'd lost his front teeth recently and couldn't have been any cuter if he'd tried.

"Last time you went to Auntie Had's, you broke a window, dipwad," Alan said.

"Come on, now," Hadley winked at Trevor and chucked Alan under the chin. "You once broke a *chair,*" she reminded him humorously, and Trev made a so-there face at his big brother.

Hadley looked at Julie. "So what's so special in Billings?"

"I want a new dress."

Hadley nodded, taking the announcement with due seriousness. Julie always wanted a new dress. She was the definitive girly-girl. "And there are no new dresses here in Lucius?"

Julie sighed. "I've seen them *all.*"

"Ahh. A problem, indeed." She looked over when the door to the office squealed open and Evie stomped out. "Hi."

Evie stopped, clearly not expecting to see Hadley standing there. The expression in her blue eyes closed. "Stu can't watch you guys today," she said.

"Then we can go with you." Julie looked delighted. Evie, however, did not.

"The kids can stay with me, if you need them to, Evie," Hadley offered. There'd been a day when her sister would have told her that she was going to Billings for some reason. A day when she'd have just dumped off the kids with no warning, in fact. But those had been days when Evie smiled, when she seemed happy and that hadn't been the case for more months than Hadley cared to acknowledge.

Evie let out a breath. "It'll have to do," she said abruptly. She leaned over and kissed her children's foreheads, one after the other, and pulled her key chain out of her pocket. "Charlie left a little bit ago for a job in Miles City. I have to pick up his father from the airport in Billings. I won't be back until after suppertime, so Charlie'll have to pick up the kids." She hurried off to her car, parked on the far side of Hadley's truck.

"Drive safely."

Evie waved but didn't look back.

Hadley looked down at the kids. At least now she knew what Evie's reasons were for the trip. Even if it did seem spur-of-the-moment. "Well. Have you had lunch?"

They all shook their heads. "Mom told us Uncle Stu would take us to Luscious," Alan said hopefully.

Hadley grinned a little. "Much as I like Luscious, I don't have time for lunch there. But you guys can have lunch at Tiff's, then you can help me bake some cookies. And Ivan is bringing out his sleigh and horses for one of my guests, so you'll get to see that, too."

Julie perked up a little at that. Trev was always happy to see her at Tiff's. And even Alan didn't look particularly peeved at the notion. So Hadley stuck her head quickly in the office. Spied Stu. "I'm taking Evie's bunch home with me. Since when is Charlie's father coming to visit?"

Stu shrugged and kept right on stacking small boxes of auto parts in their places. "Who knows? I gotta get this delivery stocked and then I'm meeting a guy about a truck I want. Couldn't have taken her kids with me if I'd wanted to."

"How is Wood's car coming along?"

He finally looked over at her. "Slow. Original parts are hard to come by, and he's insisting on them. The guy's a pain, but he does know cars. Heard you and Wendell went to church together this morning."

"Don't go there, Stu." It wouldn't take much for her anger to rear its head all over again. "I'm not doing anything *together* with Wendell."

"Aw. Come on. You're perfect for each other. He'll take good care of you, Had. He's a good guy. And you'll never have to worry that he'll treat you like Charlie treats Evie."

That was probably true, but hardly the point, as far as Hadley was concerned. She also knew that Evie didn't allow interference in her life from their brothers, no matter what. Even though Hadley's concern for her sister lately was increasing, she still envied her sister *that* ability. "Why are you so set on pushing me at him, Stu?"

He shoved a few more boxes into place, though she hardly could see how, considering how full the stock shelves were. "Maybe 'cause we want to see you happy, Had, and not flitting off somewhere again like you did last summer!"

"I didn't *flit* off. I was taking a class!"

"Class," he muttered. "Like you're gonna be some famous writer someday. Run off and find your fame and glory or something."

She pressed her palms to her stomach. "I'm not planning to run off, Stu." Not like his mother had. Beau's first wife, Evelyn, had left him with three children well before Hadley's mother had come on to the scene, and she'd never come back. "And even if I were, shoving Wendell down my throat at every corner isn't likely to make me want to stay!"

"You oughta be married and having kids of your own by now," he said gruffly.

"Well, you're thirty-five. Where's your wife and kids?" She shook her head, annoyed all over again, and not even having some sympathy for the roots of his behavior was mitigating it. "Stop messing in my life, Stu. I'm warning you."

At that, he smiled. "I'm quaking in my boots, Had."

She turned on her heel and strode out, slamming the door behind her hard enough to knock some of his carefully towered boxes right back down again. "Come on," she gestured to the kids who were waiting. "Let's go."

"Had, wait." Stu had followed her out. "Your truck is good to go." He tossed her the key. "Until next time, anyway."

Hadley caught the key and waved the kids toward her truck. Having her transportation back in working order was something, at least.

The kids piled in and she drove back to Tiff's.

Once the children had left no question that there would *not* be any leftovers from the lunch Hadley had prepared, she settled them in the kitchen with cookie makings. Before long, Mrs. Ardelle and Joanie joined them, and within an hour the smell of sugar cookies was filling the kitchen.

Hadley left them long enough to finally change out of her church clothes and into her usual jeans and a white T-shirt. Then the phone rang. She stared at it for a moment, hoping against hope that it wouldn't be Wendell. Didn't matter. She still had to answer the thing.

"I'm looking for a, um, Wood Tolliver?" The voice was feminine and very husky. A phone-sex voice.

Not that Hadley knew what a phone-sex voice sounded like. "Can you hold on for a moment and I'll see if he's in his room?"

"Of course. Thank you."

Hadley carried the cordless unit with her and knocked on Wood's door.

He yanked it open a moment later, looking a trifle harried. As if he'd been raking his fingers through his hair a few dozen times. His sleeves were shoved up his arms, and she could see papers scattered again all over his bed. She wondered anew what it was that necessitated so many notes. He seemed to have more of them than her latest manuscript attempt did. "Phone call for you."

He stared at the phone she extended as if he'd never seen one before. "Who is it?"

"I didn't ask." Some woman. Maybe the woman

you were with last night. "And I'm busy." She pushed the phone into his hand and turned away.

Unfortunately, she didn't move fast enough to miss his impatient "Hello" followed by his much *less* impatient "Hey, there, sweetheart."

Well, of course, she told herself.

Guys like Wood Tolliver naturally had a "sweetheart" somewhere. She was just fooling herself to think otherwise.

He may have kissed her, but she was the type of woman the Wendell Pierces of the world wanted, not the Wood Tollivers.

Chapter Seven

"Your sleigh, Miss Day." Hadley grinned and waved her hand at the horse-drawn sleigh waiting beside Tiff's.

Nikki Day's jaw dropped ever so slightly. "I didn't think it would be so—" She broke off and waved her ivory-gloved hand expressively.

Alan and Trev and Julie were all practically dancing around the sleigh, and she knew one of these days she was going to have to make arrangements to have *them* taken out.

"It is pretty grand," she agreed. "Every time I see it I get a little shiver." The ornate blue sleigh was like romance on gleaming runners with a plush red seat and velvet blankets with gold tassels. "And Ivan, here, will make sure his horses don't get too rambunctious, right, Ivan?"

The old man standing beside the two beautifully matched Morgans smiled and tipped his hat. ''We'll take good care of you, miss. I've been running sleigh rides in the winter and hayrides in the summer since I was a lad.''

Nikki smiled, but to Hadley it seemed forced. And the other woman's face, surrounded by a long cloud of auburn hair, looked pale. But maybe that was just because Nikki wore ivory from head to toe.

''Thank you.'' Nikki took Ivan's hand and stepped up into the sleigh and arranged a blanket over her legs. Hadley called back the kids and they reluctantly moved out of the way while Ivan climbed up onto the slanted driver's bench and picked up the reins. With a cluck of his tongue and a jingle of the horses' riggings, the sleigh set off over the open field, toward the line of trees in the distance.

''It's so pretty,'' Julie sighed. She was a dreamer. Like her aunt. Hadley hugged her narrow, young shoulders, and steered everyone back inside.

''Wash your hands before you touch any more cookies,'' she ordered when they got to the kitchen.

''What are all the cookies for?'' Alan had asked the question a few times already. He wasn't satisfied with Hadley's explanation that she'd just felt like baking. Not with Christmas and dozens of cookies still a recent memory.

But she couldn't very well tell the children they were for their mother's surprise birthday party, or there would undoubtedly *be* no surprise. ''We're making them for Grandpa Beau,'' she blatantly lied, and hoped it wasn't a terribly punishable offense.

And despite the holidays just past, she knew Evie would still appreciate the homemade storybook cookies. They'd always been her favorite.

Fortunately, the explanation seemed to satisfy Alan, who—along with his siblings—was sitting on a high stool at the counter, using paintbrushes to add colorful splotches of egg-yolk "paint" to the trays of unbaked cookies.

"That child looked peaked to me," Mrs. Ardelle observed when Hadley finished washing her own hands and sat down at the table beside Joanie. She pointed the end of the rolling pin out the back window where they could see the tail end of the sleigh gliding through the snow. "Mark my words. She's got troubles."

"She seems lonely to me," Joanie said. "And I know she's not married, 'cause I asked her." She picked up another cookie and put half of it in her mouth.

"You're supposed to be icing them, not eating them," Mrs. Ardelle said, laughter in her voice.

Joanie shrugged and smiled around her mouthful. "If Alan and Julie and Trev get to eat some, why can't I?"

Hadley added some blue piping onto the square cookie, and fashioned a little bow so it would look like a birthday gift. "I'm going to the Tipped Barrel tonight." She reached for another cookie to decorate.

Silence met her announcement.

Mrs. Ardelle finally broke it. "Excuse me, dear, but aren't they closed on Sundays?"

Hadley paused. "Well, yes, I suppose they are. Tomorrow night, then."

"But why?" Joanie's eyes were wide. "The sheriff will have a conniption fit and fall right in it."

"I don't care." And, Hadley realized, she *didn't* care if Shane disapproved. Or Stu. Or Evie or Beau or Wood. She kept trying to write stories about women, capable women, making their own way in life. How could she do that if she weren't making some similar effort in her own life? "Until this town starts seeing me as something other than the thoroughly boring and settled Hadley, nothing's going to change. Maybe Wendell's not the only one I have to convince that I *could* possess a wild side. Right?"

She looked up to see Joanie's and Mrs. Ardelle's twin expressions. "I know. I don't *look* like I belong in the Tipped Barrel." She'd figured that when she and Wood had gone there, only to find Charlie instead.

"Well," Joanie pondered. "I can help you with that. Some. I've been watching the girls doing hair at Curl up and Dye. Maybe we could do something with your hair. You know. Something a little outrageous. Sexy."

Hadley stomped out a sneaky whisper of unease. "I don't want to dye it or anything." Joanie was a receptionist at the hair salon, not a stylist.

"Joanie knows that." Mrs. Ardelle bustled over to the table and sat down, her floury hands fluttering. "But I know what she means. Fluff it up, or something. Your hair is lovely, Hadley, but it's…well, it's so—"

"Boring."

"Nice," Mrs. Ardelle finished. "You're a nice girl, Hadley, and you look like one. I'm just not sure changing your image for a night is likely to dissuade Mr. Pierce in his pursuit."

"I have to do something," Hadley muttered. "I can't seem to get my brothers from helping him along. So, unless Wendell decides himself that I'm not as suitable as he'd always figured—" She broke off when she heard the front door open, followed by a yell.

She pushed away from the table and hurried to the hall. Ivan stood there, his weathered face flushed. "Call the ambulance," he barked.

Dismay streaked through Hadley. She pointed Mrs. Ardelle toward the phone, but the woman had already yanked the receiver off the wall.

She hurriedly followed Ivan outside. "What's wrong?"

His boots clumped down the steps. "That Miss Day. She just passed out. We were nearly to the creek. Saw some deer there the other day and thought she'd enjoy seeing them. But when I looked back, she was all sort of slumped over—" He waved his hand at the sleigh, parked askew beside the house. Even the horses looked nervous, shifting and tossing their heads.

Hadley ran to the side of the sleigh and climbed up. Nikki's face was cold, her eyes closed. She was breathing, but she clearly was not waking up.

"Should we try and get her down from the sleigh?" Ivan sounded as worried as Hadley felt.

"I don't know." If something was wrong with the baby, would she be bleeding? Even though Hadley dreaded looking, she pulled back the velvet blanket. There was no visible signs of anything wrong. Which, Hadley knew, didn't mean much of anything.

She covered Nikki up again, chafing the woman's hands and nearly groaned with relief when she heard the sound of a siren. Moments later the ambulance arrived, and Palmer displaced Hadley in the confines of the sleigh as he checked Nikki over.

"Had, pull out the stretcher for me."

She was shaking like a leaf, but she ran over to the rear of the ambulance and threw open the wide door. Her hands closed over the end of the stretcher and she pulled. But it didn't move. Frustrated, she tried again.

"Here." A hand reached up and flipped the lock holding the stretcher in place. Then Wood closed his hands beside Hadley's, and they pulled the stretcher successfully from the vehicle. The legs dropped down automatically and they pushed it quickly through the skiff of snow on the sidewalk toward the sleigh from which Palmer was lifting the unconscious woman.

"Thanks. Noah's on another call already." He settled Nikki on the stretcher and fastened the safety straps carefully over her. "Hospital's gonna want her ID."

"Of course." Hadley raced up the stairs, through the house, and up to the tower. Inside Nikki's room it took her a moment to find the woman's purse, and then to make sure the wallet was inside. Then she raced back down the stairs. Palmer was already behind the wheel, clearly impatient to be on his way. She tossed him the purse through his open window, he caught it, and the ambulance drove off, siren wailing.

Hadley leaned over, pressing her palms to her stomach. "Oh, God. I should have known better than to let her go off on that sleigh ride. I didn't think she looked quite right. I should have said something to her. Done something. But I just let—"

"Stop." Wood closed his hands over her shoulders. "You're freezing. You don't have on a coat. Come inside."

She blindly followed when he urged her up the stairs. "This has never happened before. Guests don't come here and collapse, Wood."

"Shh." He pushed her into the chair in the hallway. "Take a breath before you pass out yourself."

"Auntie Hadley, are you okay?" Trevor snuck around Wood and patted the back of her head. "Why'd that lady go in the ambulance?"

She willed herself to settle down. "I'm fine, Trevor. And that lady is going to be fine, too." She hoped.

"Who's he?"

She realized her nephew was eyeing Wood. "His name is Mr. Tolliver. He's staying here while his car gets fixed. Wood, this is Evie's son, Trevor. And that—" she looked over his blond head toward the kitchen doorway "—is Julie and Alan."

Wood shifted abruptly. "Cute kids."

"Yes. You guys go on back to the kitchen and

finish the cookies with Mrs. Ardelle, okay?'' She caught that woman's eye, who nodded immediately and capably distracted the trio back to their cheerful task.

As soon as they were gone, she leaned over her knees, covering her face with her hands. ''It'll only take Palmer a few minutes to get her to the hospital. I should go over there. Someone should be called. But I don't know who.''

''What sort of information did she leave when she registered? Or made her reservation?''

''Right. Of course.'' She sat up. Pushed back her hair. ''I have home and work numbers for her.'' She went downstairs to her office and pulled out the paperwork. But since she didn't know what she'd be telling whomever she might reach, she jotted down the numbers to take with her to the hospital. She wasn't even sure if the hospital would try to reach someone for Nikki. They probably would.

Wood was waiting by the door, her parka in his hands, when she went back upstairs. She didn't look at him as she slid into the sleeves and pulled it closed around her. But when he followed her out the door after opening it for her, she couldn't help herself.

''I'm going with you,'' he said.

Her fingers closed more tightly around her keys. ''Why?'' she asked baldly.

Dane stared down at Hadley's confused face for a moment. Why, indeed? He had no love of hospitals, not having spent so much time in them recently. ''Not because I don't think you're capable on your own,'' he assured evenly. ''Now, do you want to stand here on the steps arguing about it, or shall we get going?''

For a second, he wasn't all that sure she wouldn't choose arguing, which surprised him. But she nodded, and they went to her truck, which she drove with extreme care, to the hospital. It was located on the east end of town, where the buildings didn't appear to be stuck in a fifties time warp like so much of Lucius seemed to be.

They went in through the emergency room entrance, and Hadley explained the situation to the receptionist.

Then they waited.

And waited.

And finally he couldn't sit in the molded plastic chair in the minuscule waiting room a minute longer, and he rose.

''Are you all right?'' Hadley looked up at him. The harsh light from the utilitarian fixtures overhead shined in her gleaming brown hair and ought to have made her natural features look pale. Yet there wasn't a single flaw visible in her creamy skin. And her brown eyes simply looked deeper. More liquid. ''Wood?''

''My father's in the hospital,'' he said abruptly.

Her soft eyebrows drew together, forming a tiny crease over her nose. ''Oh, Wood. I'm sorry. You must hate being here. Is it serious?''

''Enough. He's had more than one heart attack in the past two weeks.''

''Good heavens.'' She pressed her hand to her

throat. "It must be hard for you to be away from him right now."

"He's been unconscious for most of that time." He didn't want her asking why he'd leave his father at a critical time. "My sister said he's showing some signs of coming around again."

"She's the one who called Tiff's this afternoon?"

He nodded. Darby hadn't been able to reach his cell phone, because he'd been tied up on a conference call with Laura and the head of his West Coast operations. "Darby," he said after a moment. It was a family name for her. Not the one most of the world had known her by. Debra White Rutherford, the little girl who'd been kidnapped right out of a crowded elevator, outraging the entire nation.

The little girl who'd been kidnapped right out from under her brother's nose, more like.

He pushed aside the thoughts. It was being in the hospital that was doing it. Eroding his objectivity. His remoteness.

"Well, that's really good news about your father, isn't it?"

He supposed it was. Only if Roth did fully regain consciousness, he'd just continue fighting his doctors every damned inch of the way. Nobody could convince his father to do anything he didn't want to do, particularly undergoing a surgeon's scalpel.

"Yes. It should be good news."

She ran her finger back and forth over the neckline of her T-shirt. To date, it was the snuggest thing she'd worn, yet it was still too big. He had an unbidden vision of her in threads designed just for her racehorse-lean body.

"Wouldn't you rather be with him right now?" she asked, blissfully unaware of his thoughts. "You can trust Stu with your car, you know."

"My father and I don't see eye to eye," he hedged. Roth had refused the quadruple bypass the moment he'd been able to speak after his first heart attack. "So, tell me about your nephews and niece. They the only ones?"

She was distracted for a moment by the abrupt shift. "Yes. Evie had to go to Billings today and needed someone to watch them."

He wanted to ask how the oldest boy had come by the name Alan. But a nurse came out just then, asking for Hadley, and she gulped a little, and followed the nurse through the swinging double doors behind the reception area.

He pinched the bridge of his nose. Evie and Charlie's last names were Beckett. Not Michaels. It was probably too much of a stretch to think young Alan Beckett had some connection to Alan Michaels. Simply because of the similar first name?

Nevertheless, he pulled out his cell phone and went outside to the parking lot for some privacy. And there, he called Mandy Manning. If anyone could ferret out a connection, it would be her. She'd been doing investigative work for Rutherford Industries for several years now.

When he returned inside, Hadley was just coming out from the double doors again. She looked peaked and worried.

"Well?"

"It's something with her pregnancy," Hadley murmured. "The doctor didn't share too much with me, other than that she's in and out of consciousness, but the baby is stable for the moment." She pulled on her coat. "I didn't want to just leave a message on her answering machine at home. I mean, how cruel would that be to whoever gets it? I got the impression that her fiancé passed away. But I did leave a message on her work number to call me. Hopefully someone will get it since tomorrow's Monday. In the meantime, I'll just keep trying her home number."

They left the hospital, and Hadley's feet dragged to a halt. "Good grief, look at the sun. I had no idea it was so late." She looked up at him. "I guess supper's going to be late tonight. I hope nobody is too inconvenienced."

As far as Dane was concerned, she had a houseful of people perfectly capable of scaring up a meal for themselves if need be. He pulled open the truck door for her and she climbed up on the high seat, which put them pretty much eye to eye.

"You're too nice," he murmured.

She pressed her soft lips together and rolled her eyes. "It's okay. I'm a wimp. We both know it."

He shook his head. Looked out over the parking lot. In one direction he could see a brightly lit supermarket. In the other, nothing much but winter-bare land. "Do you *have* to go back to Tiff's?"

"I...why?"

He jerked his chin toward the wide-open fields. "You can practice driving out there."

Her eyes softened. "Really?"

Dammit, he was a fool. "Yeah."

She started to smile, only to shake her head. "Evie's kids. I have to—"

"Call and check."

She hesitated. Then quickly fumbled in her purse until she found her cell phone. Two minutes later she dropped the phone back into her purse. "Mrs. Ardelle said that Evie got there before Charlie did, after all. She's already picked up the children. *And* she set out supper for everyone before she left."

"There you go, then."

Hadley's fingers curled around the steering wheel and slid up and down. "She's never once helped out at Tiff's since I took it over. She just tells *me* what to do."

"Don't look a gift horse in the mouth. Your time is your own, Hadley. At least for a few minutes. Believe me. Take advantage of it."

"*Your* time isn't usually your own?"

He nearly laughed at that, only it wasn't particularly humorous. "Do you want to go driving or not?"

In answer she quickly started the engine.

"Okay, then." He rounded the truck and got in the passenger side. "Head that way."

"Out of town?"

"Yeah."

She shrugged a little and did as he asked. Within minutes, they'd left the town behind, heading in the opposite direction from where they'd collided. He pointed. "Take that access road." It was a glorified name for the narrow lane, but it was obviously well used judging by the hard-packed ruts in the dirt. The truck rocked as she slowed and turned off the highway, following his directions.

"Head toward the shelterbelt."

She gave him a sideways look. "How is this going to improve my driving?"

For some reason, he smiled. "Ye of little faith."

"Ye could be leading me down the garden path," she muttered, but she kept heading toward the line of trees he'd indicated. After a while, the road hit a little rise, and she slowed. "Hmm. I'd forgotten that was out here. How did *you* know?"

The abandoned skating rink was exactly where Mandy had described when he'd told her to find a suitable place for some behind-the-wheel. Not that he'd really intended to make use of it.

"Yeah, I knew about it. Come on. It's gonna be completely dark in a half hour."

She drove down toward the abandoned rink, stopping for him to get out and drag open the gate. It listed sadly to one side, falling right off its hinges. The rest of the wooden fence surrounding the clearing was mostly still intact, and inside the ground was fairly level, with only a thin coat of snow.

When he returned to the truck, he told her to slide over, and got behind the wheel himself. She fastened her safety belt when he did. He put the old truck in gear and drove it around the perimeter of the rink.

"I'll give Stu credit," he said when he stopped

two feet away from where he'd begun. ''The truck handles better than I'd have expected. Okay, your turn. Only I want you to drive on the inside of the tracks I just made.''

''I have to unpeel my fingers first.'' She eyed him. ''You weren't kidding about the racing thing.''

''That wasn't even close to racing.'' Amused, he leaned over himself and unclipped her seat belt. ''Without some weight in the truck bed, we'd be all over the place if I really punched it. Just because I was going more than five miles an hour is no reason to panic.''

''Five? More like seventy-five. And I wasn't panicking.'' Her voice was faintly huffy. ''I was just…surprised.''

''Right.'' He climbed out and rounded the truck and got back in the passenger side when she slid over behind the wheel. ''You can still see the tire tracks, right?'' She nodded, fastening herself in once more. ''Put your wheel on the inner track and follow it around. Go as slow as you want.''

She did as he asked, missing the track by a good two feet. He pointed out a few corrections. Showed her how to gauge her distance more accurately. ''How long have you driven this thing?'' he asked when she finally managed to hit the mark and stay there.

She was sitting up impossibly straight, peering tensely over the hood of the truck, working hard on keeping her alignment with the round track. ''Forever.''

They made it around the rink once. ''Okay. Do it

again. But stop making such hard work out of it. You know where your bearings are. Trust them.''

She deliberately sat back in the seat. Loosened her death grip on the steering wheel. ''This is embarrassing,'' she muttered. ''I ought to be able to drive in a circle without making a mess of it.''

He covered her fingers for a moment with his. ''You're not making a mess. Now stop thinking so much and just drive.'' He moved his hand away.

''It was *not* thinking about my driving that landed your car into a tree,'' she reminded him. But she flexed her fingers once more and took the circle perfectly.

And when he told her to speed up, she did that, too, until they were virtually flying around the ring. She forgot being uptight about every bump of the tires, and started relaxing into the motion of the vehicle. He showed her how to control a skid, and he even had her drive the entire circle in reverse, with nothing lighting her way but the moon overhead and the red glow of her taillights.

''Nothing to it,'' he said when she put her foot on the brake with finality and waved her hands that she'd had enough.

She shifted in her seat, facing him. ''Nothing to it?'' She laughed. ''I'm positively worn-out! How long have we been at it?''

He didn't even look at his watch. Couldn't seem to look away from her. He smiled. ''Long enough. The only thing you need, Hadley, is some confidence.''

''Stu's always telling me to get my head out of

my imagination and pay closer attention to what I'm supposed to be doing.''

''Nothing wrong with some imagination,'' he murmured. God knew his was running riot at that particular moment. It had been a long time—a *very* long time—since he'd sat in a parked vehicle with an entrancing woman beside him. But as long as he kept his thoughts to the realm of make-believe, there was no harm done.

''Hmm.'' She didn't sound so sure. ''How *did* you know about this place? I'd completely forgotten it was even out here.''

''I asked.''

She waited for a moment for him to elaborate. Warm air from the heater vents whispered over them. ''Well. It was really sweet of you. And I do appreciate it.'' She smiled. Then laughed and leaned forward, throwing her arms around his neck. ''Thank you.'' She kissed his cheek.

Dane's fingers flexed against her waist.

She went still. Pulled her head back a little to look at him through eyes as dark as midnight. ''Wood?''

He exhaled roughly. Deliberately moved his hands away from her. ''You need to get over this notion that I'm remotely sweet.''

Her palm lifted and stroked down his cheek in a gentle motion. ''But you are.''

He grabbed her fingers. ''No.''

''Wood—''

''Don't call me that.''

She blinked slowly. ''Why?''

Jesus. He was losing it. ''Nothing. You…nothing.''

He wanted to hear his real name on her lips, and that wasn't going to happen. She couldn't abide liars, and he couldn't take a chance on letting the Rutherford name being recognized in Lucius. If Alan Michaels *was* in town somewhere, or heading there, as they suspected, he'd run for certain if Dane's name came out.

"Don't frown," she murmured. "What are you so angry over? Are you worried about your father? Do you need help getting back to see him? If it's money, I can—"

"No." God. She was going to offer him money. And the idea of it was so ironic it was nearly laughable. "I don't need money. I don't need to see him."

"You shouldn't let disagreements keep you apart. He's your father."

"He'd rather find an early grave than go under the knife," Dane said flatly.

Her fingers somehow managed to get out of his grip, and turned the tables, squeezing gently. "Maybe he's afraid."

"Maybe he's the most controlling and stubborn person to ever walk the planet." And he really didn't want to discuss Roth. He wanted to press her against the seat and sink into her for a few dozen decades. "What's your dad like? A minister, right?"

She nodded. "Beau. He's great. I couldn't love him more if he were my natural father." Her voice was soft. Little more than a whisper.

"Yeah?" Whisper or not, he was barely listening, anyway. Her lips were less than a breath from his.

"Yeah."

He closed the small gap. Oh, yeah. Her lips were soft. Cool despite the truck's heater. He reached past her and shoved the gearshift into Park.

Which only pushed her closer against him. Her arms slid around his shoulders, fingers delving beneath the collar of his shirt and back up again. She murmured his name.

Wood's name.

Right then he didn't care.

He tangled his fingers in her hair and deepened the kiss. She moaned a little, and the sound shot straight to his head like the strongest moonshine. The safety belts were strangling them. He unclipped them both. Hauled her onto his lap the moment they were freed.

Her silky, fragrant hair drifted over him as he slid his arms beneath her jacket. Good intentions flew out the window, and he didn't even give them a second thought.

He only cared about making the moment go on. His fingers skimmed beneath the hem of her shirt. Found the warmth of her spine.

She gasped and dropped her head to his shoulder, her clutching hands kneading his waist through his heavy sweater. She rocked against him, and he let out a groaning laugh. "I haven't had sex in a car in a long time, sweetness. I've got a condom in my wallet, but it's so damn old, I don't know if the thing's even safe."

She shifted her knee on the seat beside him, and her breasts thrust so easily into his hand. "I haven't had sex ever, so—" She broke off when he froze. "Wood?"

He dumped her off his lap. "You're a virgin." He thumped his head back against the seat. Of course she was a virgin. She was innocence on mile-long legs. Didn't matter that she was twenty-damn-seven.

"It's not catching," she said after a moment, and he swore under his breath. So much for finesse.

"It's not—" He scrubbed his hands down his face, willing his body to cool it. "It's not that."

She drew back her legs until they were no longer sprawling over his. "Oh?" A wealth of defensiveness filled that one small word.

"I don't want to take advantage of you, Hadley."

The air was cooling by degrees and it had nothing to do with the temperature outside the vehicle. "How big of you."

"Dammit. Look. You're a nice gir—woman. You're a nice woman. And I…am not all that nice a man. Okay?"

She put her hands on the steering wheel. "Don't make excuses, Wood. It's insulting to us both. Honesty is no sin. Just admit it. I don't—" she lifted her shoulders in some manner meant to convey God knew what "—do it for you."

How could she turn him on and infuriate him all within one breath?

"Do it," he repeated. He was hard as a rock. A lamentably frequent occurrence where she was concerned, which was more than a little annoying for any guy past seventeen. "You cannot possibly be that naive." But she *could.*

He put his hand under her chin and deliberately turned her face toward his. "Believe me, Hadley, you're more than fine. But I don't get involved with anyone who can get hurt.''

She eyed him, her expression plain.

She didn't believe him. And after a long moment, she turned to face forward. Then she drove back to town.

If he'd have known how to break that hurt silence, he would have.

But he didn't.

Chapter Eight

"Michaels hasn't used his credit card in two weeks," Mandy Manning said, setting a squat drink in front of Dane. She moved down the bar to deliver the rest of her tray's contents, then returned. "And I didn't find any connection between him and Evie and Charlie Beckett, yet. Maybe Michaels was never intending to come to Lucius at all," she suggested.

Dane twisted the glass in a circle, staring at the scarred bar. Since the incident last night, he'd been more determined than ever to locate Alan Michaels. As soon as he saw some justice served, he'd leave Hadley Golightly and her virginal self behind.

Unfortunately, Dane wasn't sure he'd ever pick up the man's trail again if he wasn't in Lucius.

Which was not acceptable.

"How'd the lunatic ever get a credit card in the first place?"

Mandy shrugged. It wasn't the first time Dane had expressed that opinion. "There aren't many unfamiliar people in Lucius." She kept her voice low, for his ears only. "If the guy was a drinker, he'd have been in here, and he hasn't. If he were buying food, he'd have gone to one of the stores here. He hasn't. I think the guy's gone to ground, Dane. Who knows why he was so fascinated with Lucius while he was in the loony bin. He's nuts. That's why he was there in the first place. Be happy that the stuff he found on Darby was years old with no info about her whereabouts now."

She leaned her elbows on the bar and looked him in the eye. "Not that I'm opposed to earning my fee here, my friend, but you might want to start thinking twice about the cost."

"Money." He snorted softly, dismissing the idea of it. And he wasn't worried about his sister. Roth had his usual cadre of bodyguards around, which would extend to Darby, as well. And even more so, she had her husband, Garrett, by her side.

Dane knew his brother-in-law was more than capable of protecting Darby. It was up to Dane to right the wrong he'd been responsible for all those years ago.

Mandy just tsked and pressed her hand over his. "There are different sorts of *cost*," she reminded. Then she straightened and picked up her tray once more. "Tips have been good lately." She smiled faintly and set off to deliver and take a fresh round of orders, her short, ruffled skirt swaying.

Dane turned on the stool and leaned his elbows back on the bar, his drink held loosely between his fingers. His gaze drifted over the occupants of the Tipped Barrel. Mostly locals. Mostly regulars. There was a pretty steady stream of people coming. Going. It might be a Monday night, but the bar was popular.

And Alan Michaels had looked the place up on the Internet before he'd escaped from the loony bin, as Mandy liked to call it.

He was still hoping some connection might come up between Michaels and Charlie Beckett. Thanks to the free-and-easy gossip around Lucius, he knew the guy's father had just come to town. There'd never been a record of Michaels having had any children, but there had been a record of a very brief marriage years before the kidnapping. Mandy had tried locating the ex-wife—Hannah Michaels—but had had no success. It was probably a long shot, but maybe Beckett's long-absent father was Alan Michaels.

He lifted the glass of scotch and sipped.

Then nearly choked when the door opened again and a slender brunette stepped inside, blowing all other thoughts out of his mind for a stunned moment.

She paused inside the doorway, as if she were gathering her nerve. Then she tossed back her head a little, shrugged out of the tight leather coat she wore and strode inside, sailing past the pool tables as if she'd been striding around on beer-sticky floors wearing four-inch-spiked heels her entire life.

He shoved his drink on the bar and took an intersecting path to catch her. "Hadley." He curled his fingers around her elbow. Her shirt covered her from neck to wrists, and the fabric felt slippery beneath his grasp. And while the cut might seem modest, the fabric was not.

Except for a hint of gray shimmer, the thing was sheer.

Completely sheer.

Completely showing off the seductive black bra she wore beneath it.

Now he knew what lay beneath those enveloping clothes she wore. And so did every other person present in the bar.

Perfection.

"What do you think you're doing?"

She shook back her hair again. Part of it was twisted up in some sexy knot atop her head, and the rest flowed around her shoulders in a disarray that was meant to put every man who saw it in mind of spreading it across a pillow.

Or a truck seat.

"I'm going to have a drink," she said brightly. Very brightly. As if she were keeping that brightness up by nerve and willpower. "What are *you* doing here? Is this where you've been hanging out all day?"

"I told you the other night the Tipped Barrel was no place for you." He tried to draw her toward the door, but she did a little shimmy and escaped like an agile little fish. "Hadley."

She turned on her heel and strode over to the bar. When she reached in the back pocket of her jeans for her money, Dane could practically hear the eye-balls popping out of the male customers.

Where had she gotten that outfit? The shirt was overtly sexy. The jeans—the *body* they outlined with loving detail—were nothing short of miraculous.

He didn't know what aggravated him more. The fact that he was salivating over her or the fact that there were other men doing exactly the same thing.

She'd worked her money free and plunked several bills on the gleaming bar. Dane slid between her and the guy next to her who'd suddenly started looking awake. "You don't drink," he reminded.

"There's lots of things I haven't done," she said pointedly. "And look where it's gotten me." The bartender hadn't gotten to her yet, and she leaned over the bar, waving at him. "Hey, Billy. Don't take all night now, okay?" She tilted her head back and eyed Dane. "Billy and I go way back. I used to help him with English composition in high school."

She'd done something to her eyes. Put makeup on.

He was used to women who were masters at the art of using cosmetics.

No woman he'd ever wanted to date, had dated, or even bedded, had possessed eyes like Hadley.

He didn't need a drink. He needed a damn dunking in a snow bank.

The guy beside him rustled, trying to move around Dane and closer to Hadley. Dane casually planted his elbow in his ribs and gave the scum a direct look.

He made a face, but turned back to his bowl of peanuts and beer.

"If this is about what happened last night—"

"You mean what *didn't* happen? Please." She waved her hand. "All forgotten."

He believed that about as much as he believed the moon was made of cheese. "Hadley—"

"Hey, Hadley." Billy the bartender stopped in front of them. "You're looking, uh, fine. Real fine. What can I get you?"

"Nothing."

She gave Dane a narrow look when he answered the bartender for her, then turned her attention back to good ol' Billy. "Sex on the beach," she said promptly.

Billy's eyebrows went up, but he nodded and turned around, grabbing vodka and peach schnapps in a smooth move.

"What'd you do? Look up drinks on the Internet?"

"I have a book, actually," she said coolly. "Research. Do you have a problem with that?"

"I have a lot of problems. All of them have to do with what you think you're doing in here. You want to scare off Wendell? Honey, he finds out what you look like in those jeans and that *non*shirt, and you're never gonna shake the guy."

Her lashes drifted down and her lips pursed softly. "Something wrong with the way I look?"

He snorted. "Did you practice the pout in the mirror?"

She tossed her head again and faced the bar once more when Billy set the drink on a coaster and slid it in front of her. She smiled and paid him, then picked up the drink.

Dane was heartened to see her hesitate. But then she took a hefty swig.

And couldn't quite contain a gasp.

"Serves you right," he muttered. "Have you had enough fun, now?"

"I haven't even begun," she assured him, and took another drink. Slightly more gingerly. "Go play pool or something, why don't you? I don't need a baby-sitter."

"Sweetness, in that outfit, you need a jailer. What would you do if your brothers saw you like this?"

"Why should I have to do anything?" she defended. "I'm a grown woman. And despite opinions to the contrary, I'm over the age of consent. I run my own business and if I want to go to a bar, I'll darned well go to a bar!" Her voice had risen.

"You tell 'm, sugar." The man on the other side of her lifted his beer mug in a salute.

Hadley pressed her shining pink lips together for a moment. "Right." Then she clinked her glass to his. "Right," she said even more surely. She lifted the glass, and tossed back more than half of it. "Oh. That just starts tasting better as it goes down, doesn't it? Billy." She leaned over the bar again and flagged him down. "Give me another one of these."

"You're going to regret it," Dane warned.

She folded her arms on the bar and leaned toward him. "Well, that'll be my problem, won't it? Besides, don't people usually regret what they *don't* do, versus what they do...do?" She grinned, looking thoroughly amused with herself.

"Half a drink and you're already drunk."

''Don't be so stuffy.'' She patted his arm and curled her hand around her glass, finishing it off quickly. She looked around the bar. Billy set her second drink beside her and she picked it up. ''I'm going to dance.''

''A little Dutch courage goes a long way.'' He slid the fresh drink out of her fingers. But if he'd hoped to stop her, he'd failed. She and her lethal high heels clicked their way through the tables toward the square floor. The live music was nothing but pure honky-tonk. And as soon as she was within three feet of the dance floor, there were that many guys eager to swing her on out.

Dane shoved her drink back onto the bar. He eyed Billy. ''The next one better be a virgin, no matter what she orders. Clear?''

''That oughta be up to Hadley, don't you think?''

Dane gave him a hard look. Billy swallowed. Nodded. ''Yeah, okay. Whatever.'' He headed on down the bar, grabbing a mug and pulling on the tap.

Mandy hurried past, giving him a curious look as she picked up another tray of orders. On the dance floor, Hadley was dancing as if her life depended on it, and he wondered what kind of book could have taught her how to move like that. Maybe it was just one of those gifts of hers lurking under the surface.

He exhaled roughly. The woman *was* an adult, he reminded himself. He picked up her drink and tasted it. Winced at the combination of fruit juices and alcohol.

A circle had formed around the dance floor, a mass of stomping feet and clapping hands. Balls clacked together on the pool tables. The music was getting louder, the cigarette smoke thicker.

He should've just kissed Hadley in her kitchen when she'd asked. She'd be satisfied that she was dissuading Wendell in his pursuit, and she wouldn't be out on the dance floor dancing with a half-dozen different guys at once.

He raked his fingers through his hair. How many times had he heard Darby complaining about Roth's overprotective behavior where she was concerned? About his manipulations in her life? She'd virtually run away for a good portion of a year in order to escape it.

Hadley had her own version of that same struggle, in her brothers.

But try as he might, he couldn't leave her out there on that dance floor. She might not mind getting leered at, pawed at in her chaotic pursuit for excitement, but he sure in hell did.

He worked his way through the increasingly tighter clutch of people inside the bar. You'd think they were giving away free beer judging by the numbers of people who kept crowding into the place. There was not one square foot of dance floor left unoccupied.

And then there was Hadley. Right in the middle, a drink in her hand as she twirled in circles.

"Okay, sweetness. Enough fun for one night." He slid his arm around her waist, halting her in her tracks.

She bumped flat against him, her breath coming

out in a little *oof*. Her breasts were pressed up snug against his chest.

"All you had to do was ask," she said, and started to loop her hands around his neck, only to spill half the drink on the floor. "Oh." She looked down at the mess. But it quickly disappeared under the shuffling of feet, and she shrugged. Her smile was fuzzy.

And, of course, the hard-driving music just had to stop right then.

Half the dancers exited the floor only to be just as quickly replaced by others, wanting their music and right now. A few catcalls filled the air. Taped music quickly replaced the live as the band members took a break, tromping down off the small stage.

Dane took advantage of the commotion and slid the glass out of Hadley's lax fingers. He pulled her other hand from where it kept sliding up to toy with his hair. He sniffed the glass. Rum and coke this time. She was going to have a helluva hangover.

"Come on." He grabbed her wrist and pulled her inexorably from the floor. "Time to go."

"Whoa, there, buddy. If the lady wants to stay, that's her business, know what I mean?"

Dane's jaw tightened. He looked at the man who'd stopped in front of him. The semi truck, he corrected. The guy was huge. He hadn't been in a brawl in more years than he could count. But he still recognized the scent of one just waiting in the wings. And the Tipped Barrel was ripe with it. "She's my business," he said smoothly. "Know what I mean?"

Hadley crowded up against his back. He didn't know if it was an attempt at distracting him—which wasn't going to work no matter how sweet her body felt against his—or if she'd finally had enough of this particular run for independence.

"I know you ain't got no ring on her finger. So, seems to me she oughta choose for herself."

Someone jostled hard against Hadley, and Dane turned, steadying her.

Semi truck clapped a meaty hand on Dane's shoulder. "Don't turn away from me, man. You and me, we're having a discussion."

Dane shrugged off the guy's hand. "Discuss it with someone who gives a damn." He pulled Hadley after him.

Semi had other ideas, though, and grabbed Hadley's other hand. "I think she wants to stay."

Dane stopped. Eyed the guy's big fingers touching Hadley. "Let her go."

"She don't want me to." Semi leered, his gaze not so clearly focused on Hadley's chest. "Do you, baby?"

"My brother's the sheriff," she hissed, twisting her wrist.

Semi laughed. He simply scooped her around the waist and started to haul her closer.

Dane's fist popped out and caught the guy square in the jaw, snapping his head back. His eyes rolled, and he went down into the dance floor throng without ceremony.

Hadley squealed and jumped out of the way. She stood over the man's enormous body for a moment. "Is he hurt?"

Dane sure in hell hoped so. He dropped the sturdy,

squat glass his hand had been wrapped around on a nearby table. "Let's go."

This time Hadley didn't argue.

Probably because Semi was already starting to stir.

Before they reached the door, Mandy shoved Hadley's coat that she'd left near the bar into his hands. "Nice hook," she murmured, sounding amused.

Dane nudged Hadley out into the cold night air and knew by the way her head snapped back a little that it had hit her hard after the stifling confines inside the bar.

She pressed her hand to her head, her steps definitely wobbling. And he didn't think it was because of the come-love-me heels she was wearing. He stuffed her arms into the leather coat and pulled it closed, zipping it up. His knuckles brushed against her as he worked. "Whose coat?"

"Joanie's."

Figures. Despite her advanced pregnancy, Dane knew the other woman was a half-pint compared to Hadley's leggy build. No wonder the coat fit so closely.

"And her shirt. She did my hair, too," Hadley murmured when he finished zipping.

"Great." He put his arm around her and looked around the parking lot. Her truck was pretty easy to spot, and he headed that way. He'd already taken her keys out of the coat pocket. "Remind me to thank her."

"And Mrs. Ardelle helped, too."

"Did she now?"

Her legs bobbled as they wove between vehicles.

Dane swore under his breath. "You're gonna break an ankle on those things."

She stopped cold and leaned over to look at her shoes. Only to lose her balance and stumble forward.

Dane caught her. Picked her up and tossed her over his shoulder.

"Hey!" She slapped his butt. Hard. "Whadare-yadoing?"

"Taking you home. Now stop hitting me or I might let you go back and keep the semi truck company back there."

"Semi—Oh. Yeah." She giggled. "He was kinda big. You sure landed him a good one, though. Shane woulda been proud."

Her arms slid around his waist and grabbed his belt buckle. He could feel her head bouncing against his rear and his steps faltered for a moment.

The truck. Get to the bloody truck.

"I'll sleep better tonight knowing that," he assured dryly.

"Wood?"

He unlocked the truck. "Yeah?"

"I'm a little dizzy up here."

He opened the door and slid her off his shoulder and, boneless, she collapsed on the seat. She pushed her hair out of her face when he reached around her, fastening her into the safety belt. "I wish you hadn't stopped last night," she whispered, her voice husky.

Inviting or not, she'd had too much to drink. Hell, one sip for her was too much.

"Someday you'll thank me." His arid tone escaped her. He closed the door on her and went around to the driver's side. By the time he'd made the short drive back to Tiff's, she was practically lying across the bench seat, her head only an inch from his thigh.

He parked on the street in front of the house. "I can walk," she insisted when he opened her door to help her out.

"Okay." Carrying her was only so much self-inflicted torture, anyway. "Walk."

She set out. Her ankles wobbled. He grabbed her by the waist and half carried, half walked her up the steps and inside the silent, dark house.

"Is...oops. Too loud." She dropped her voice to a husky whisper. "Is it that late?"

"Past everyone's bedtime," he assured. "Even yours." He nudged the carpet runner back into place when her dragging feet pulled it askew. "Almost there." He turned down the hallway toward their two bedrooms.

"Are you gonna kiss me g'night?"

"No."

She pouted. "But I like your kisses."

"Too bad. Along with virgins, I don't mess with women too drunk to know what they're doing."

She pulled away from him, walking more or less under her own steam. She bumped into the wall. "Shh. Don't wanna wake anybody." Her voice was pure earnestness.

"Right." He redirected her shuffle toward her bedroom door, but it was locked. "Have the key?"

She frowned. Thought about it. "I dunno. I think I, um, forgot. Joanie was doing my hair. And Mrs.

Ardelle was, um…'' She wrinkled her nose. ''What were we talkin' 'bout?''

''Come on.'' He stepped back to his own door and opened it, nudging her through.

She entered just far enough to sit down with a plop on the side chair set against the wall. ''You were a virgin once,'' she observed abruptly.

Dane ignored her and went into the bathroom and stuck his knuckles under a stream of cold water. It stung like a bitch.

''Well, you were,'' she said in what she probably figured was a loud whisper.

He looked at his reflection in the mirror. The entire evening had taken on a surreal cast. He shut off the water and shook his hand, looking back into his room. Her legs were stretched out in front of her and she was leaning over the wooden arm, her head propped on her hand.

''We all start out that way,'' he agreed blandly. He didn't know why he didn't just trot her through the connecting bathroom and dump her on her bed. She'd sleep it off, and probably be embarrassed for a month of Sundays if she happened to remember any of the night's events.

''Her boss is coming.''

He tossed that around for a moment. Shook his head. ''Who's boss?''

''Nikki Day's.'' She yawned, covering her mouth with the back of her hand. ''At least I think he's her boss.'' Her eyes closed. ''He said not to worry. He'd take care of everything.''

''There you go, then. No need to worry.

"The nurses wouldn't tell me anything." She yawned again. "I'm not family. But I couldn't even reach her family, 'cause I don't know who they are."

"What'd your brother say about it?"

"Nothing, 's long 's her boss is coming."

He eyed her. "If you sink any lower in that chair, you're gonna end up on the floor."

She waved lazy hands. Pulled herself up a little, took a breath and pushed herself up from the chair. The momentum carried her forward a few feet until she bumped into him. "You always smell so good," she murmured, and dropped her head against his chest.

He caught her as she turned boneless. "Hadley?" He tilted back her head.

She was sound asleep.

And that's what he got for not putting her to bed more quickly. He lifted her and carried her through the bathroom, trying not to knock her dangling feet into anything as he turned the old-fashioned crystal doorknob.

Only that door was as locked as the hallway door had been.

He cursed under his breath and carried her back to his room, settling her on the bed. "Serve you right if I let you sleep on that horse-hair settee in the parlor." She lay there, as quiet and still as the moonlight shining on the snow outside his window.

And he was no gentleman. *He* wasn't going to seek out that particular piece of furniture, either.

He pulled off her skinny-heeled boots and tossed them on the floor. Feeling anything but good-natured about it, he yanked the quilt from the other side of the bed and tossed it over her. Then he ditched his own boots and shirt, grabbed the extra blanket she'd been so careful to leave for him, and lay down on what was left of the bed.

He might as well be comfortable. But there was no way in hell he'd find any restful sleep with Hadley Golightly occupying his bed.

Chapter Nine

There was a crop of cotton growing in her mouth.

Hadley groaned and buried her head a little farther under the pillow. But the light still managed to penetrate, seeming to sear right through her eyelids. She would have groaned again, except that her head was still reverberating from the first one.

She moved, cautiously stretching out her legs. The realization that she was still dressed in her jeans came slowly. Even more slowly did it dawn on her that she wasn't twisted up in her soft chenille comforter but a quilt that verged more on the crisp side.

She gingerly pulled the pillow off her head and peeled open an eyelid.

Wood was sleeping beside her.

In her mind she jumped right off the bed. The spirit might have been willing, but the flesh was simply incapable.

And opening her other eyelid didn't magically make his apparition fade, either.

He slept on his back, one arm tossed above his head, throwing the muscles in his shoulder into sharp definition. A dark blur of whiskers softened his jaw, but not his appeal. A thick lock of warm-brown hair fell forward over his forehead, obscuring the bandage there. The pale-blue blanket she'd left for him was bunched about his waist. A whorl of hair sprinkled over his hard chest, forming a vee that narrowed and thinned as it neared the barrier of soft wool.

She curled her fingers into the pillow, but it was a poor substitute for the flesh and bone they wanted to explore.

She tried turning on her side, but was trapped by the twists of the quilt around her. She tried remembering what had transpired at the Tipped Barrel the night before, but the details were definitely fuzzy. Caused by that second—or was it third?—drink she'd had, no doubt.

Whatever. Thinking too closely about it just made her head hurt even more.

But instinct was still alive and well, and it was telling her to get out of that bed before the man awakened. Before she had to look him in the face and not shrivel away in mortification.

She cautiously moved her foot, searching for the edge of the quilt. No luck. One of her arms was free, but the other was pinned beneath her. She felt like a turkey trussed for Thanksgiving.

She slowly worked a knee upward, giving herself a little leverage. The edge of the quilt was obviously trapped underneath her.

"Stop bouncing." Wood turned on his side and threw his arm over her cocooned self. "Be still."

She froze. Peered at him over a fold of quilted log-cabin squares.

His eyes were slits of pale blue between his thick, narrowed lashes. "I finally manage to go to sleep and you start doing gymnastics thirty minutes later." His voice was husky, and shivers danced down her spine.

"I'm sorry. I think it's late. I have to get up."

"You have to stop squirming around." He scooped her, quilt and all, right next to him and dropped his jean-clad leg over hers.

And she'd thought the blanket had pinned her pretty effectively.

"Your regulars can get their own damn breakfast for once."

"But—"

He put his hand over her mouth, sighing mightily. "Shh. Be still."

She blinked at him over his hand. And remained silent.

"Good," he murmured after a moment, and moved his hand from her mouth to push the tumbled mess of her hair away from her cheek. With his fingers still threaded through her hair, he closed his eyes again.

In minutes his fingers went lax.

Something sweet flowed through her, warm as summer honey, and she lay there far longer than she ought to. From somewhere in the house she heard a telephone ring. The occasional sound of a door. The murmur of a voice, the muffled weight of a footstep.

There'd be no breakfast waiting in the dining room this morning, but nobody seemed to be sending up an alarm over it, either.

Eventually, however, she couldn't lie there staring at him, no matter how abundantly, beautifully masculine he was.

She turned toward him this time and managed to free the elusive edge of the quilt. Then she slid off the bed, wavered for a moment when her head felt in danger of exploding, then cautiously tiptoed to the bathroom.

She shut the door and nearly scared two years off her life with her own reflection.

The shadows and liner that Mrs. Ardelle had applied to Hadley's eyes so carefully the night before was smeared halfway down her cheeks. She looked like a raccoon after a hard night. And her hair…mercy, her hair looked like a dust mop.

Moving as quickly as her tender nerve endings allowed, she washed her face and brushed her teeth and hair. But when she tried to open the door to her bedroom, the knob didn't budge.

Muttering under her breath, she tiptoed back into Wood's bedroom, feeling herself flush just from the sight of the tumbled bedding, and opened the door to the hallway.

Shane stood out there, his lifted hand clearly poised to knock on her door. She hastily backed up a step, intending to close Wood's door again, but that would have been too easy. Oh, no. Shane-with-the-hearing-of-a-bat turned and looked at her.

His hand slowly lowered to his side, and his face darkened. She hurriedly stepped into the hallway and pulled the door shut behind her but knew it was too little, too late.

He'd obviously seen the bed. And Wood in it.

"What are you doing here, Shane?"

His jaw canted to one side, then centered again. "What are you doing *there,* Hadley?" His voice was pleasant.

She crossed her arms, determined to avoid feeling defensive and pretty much failing miserably. "I run Tiff's, remember?"

He tapped his cowboy hat against the side of his leg. "Offering pretty personal service, then, are you?"

She flushed. "That's crude."

"And you're naive." He jerked his chin at the door behind her. "You think he's gonna stick around Lucius once his business here is done?"

She didn't think anything of the sort. More's the pity. But she wasn't going to give Shane the satisfaction of seeing just how much she already dreaded Wood's eventual departure. "You haven't said what you're doing here." Every word she spoke felt like a spike driving into her skull.

"You didn't show up to help out at the church this morning. Dad got worried. He called here but nobody had seen hide nor tail of you." His gaze cut to the door behind her. "Almost nobody."

Dismay congealed inside her. "I completely forgot."

"Tell that to Dad."

"I will."

"You can also explain what the hell you were doing at the Tipped Barrel last night." His lips twisted. "As if I couldn't guess. Is this the kind of effect he—" he jerked his chin toward the door "—is going to have on you? 'Cause I gotta tell you, turnip, he's not what you think. He's hiding something, sure as the sun rises. And how many times have I told you to stay outta the Barrel? I busted a woman just the other day for solicitation there. *Nice* girls don't go there. You think you're gonna find whatever the hell you want in life by going there?"

Hadley could feel herself shrinking down by the yard. She heard the door behind her open and wished the ground would swallow her whole. She really, *really* didn't need Wood witnessing her brother giving her a dressing down.

She chanced a look over her shoulder at him and, despite the situation, felt her stomach hollow out all over again at the sight of him—rumpled, shirtless and positively dangerous to a woman's heart.

He ran the palm of his hand up her arm and cupped her shoulder, absorbing the surprised jerk she gave. "She's a grown woman, Sheriff," he said smoothly. "Think it's her business where she chooses to go."

She shot him a quick look even though the abrupt

motion hurt. If her beleaguered memory served, his opinion the night before had been quite different.

"Including your room," Shane finished, his voice hard.

"Shane! That's not what—"

"If that's her decision," Wood spoke over her and he might just as well have waved a red flag.

Shane's eyes went flinty and he advanced. "I warned you," he said softly. "You hurt my sister and—"

"Stop!" Hadley pressed her palms flat against both men's chests, horrified at the thickening tension between them. "*What* is wrong with you, Shane? And *you*—" she glared at Wood "—aren't any better. Egging each other on like a couple of bulldogs! *You* know nothing happened between us whatsoever, because you won't let it." She turned and eyed her brother. "You may be the sheriff here, and I may love you dearly, but you have absolutely no business making any kind of judgments about how I spend my time or with whom I spend it! And maybe I'm more than a little tired of everyone being so darned sure I'm so *nice*. The only one who deserves any kind of apology or explanation is Dad since he's the one I let down this morning. A first, I might add."

Irritated and feeling in dire need of dunking her head in soft cotton and leaving it there, she stomped over to her room. The perfect exit was definitely foiled, however, when the door wouldn't budge.

She turned on her heel and walked past the men again, daring them with a pointed look to say one word, just one word, and went through the kitchen and downstairs to her office.

Her ring of keys for all the locks at Tiff's was in her rarely used desk. She had to hunt for a few minutes before she closed her fingers over them, and the old heavy telephone rang shrilly while she was looking. She groaned aloud and snatched it up, if only to stop the noise.

It was Wendell calmly asking if it were true that she'd been in a bar fight the night before.

She almost sat down in the old-fashioned desk chair but feared she'd probably want to stay there hiding for the rest of the day if she did. "It wasn't a fight, Wendell." It would probably be better to let Wendell think it was, but she just couldn't make herself lie. "Not exactly."

"As long as you weren't hurt, dear. That's not a place for a girl like you. I'm taking a short trip to Colorado for the weekend. I wondered if you'd like to go? There's a bird-watchers' convention that I think you'd really enjoy."

Hadley stared blindly at the desk. "You want me to go away with you for the weekend."

"Well, yes. I don't mean anything suggestive, Hadley. I know you're not like that."

So much for her expedient little plan.

She pressed her palm to her throbbing forehead. She was never drinking again. "I don't think so, Wendell. Thank you for the invitation, though. I really have to go now." She hung up as soon as he'd expressed a disappointed goodbye.

Then, before her misery grew any more, she

quickly called Beau and apologized. He, at least, didn't have any lectures to give her, for which she was grateful. Then she wrapped her hand around the keys to silence their clinking together and dragged herself back upstairs.

Wood and Shane were *still* standing outside his door looking at each other with mental daggers. Well, fine. Couple of idiot men is what they were. And she was the idiot woman who just wanted everyone to get along. Because she was such a *nice* girl.

A nice girl. A comfortable girl. An old-socks sort of girl. An untouchable virgin.

Heaven help her.

She unlocked her door and went inside, giving it a good slam behind her. Satisfaction was stomped out, though, by the sharp pain that exploded inside her head at the noise. She pressed her hands to her temples and shuffled to the bed, dropping down on the piles of discarded clothing still lying there from the previous night.

When the door slammed behind Hadley, the sheriff looked at Dane. "That car may not be stolen, but I haven't given up on you," he warned. "This is my town. My family. Whatever your real business here is, finish it up fast and move on."

"Keep pressing Hadley under your thumb and you're gonna lose her altogether."

"You're threatening me?"

Dane wasn't fazed. "Sharing my experience," he said evenly. "You want to protect someone you love. I understand that. But you can't run their life, either.

Sooner or later, you'll either break them or they'll rebel. I don't figure you really want either one of those things to happen.''

The other man was silent for a moment. ''What's your story, Tolliver? And don't think I believe that's your real name.''

''Think what you want about me.'' Dane knew the man couldn't do anything about his suspicions. Not as long as he broke no laws. ''But lighten up on Hadley.''

Shane's gaze shifted to her closed door. ''She's a dreamer. Always writing in those notebooks of hers. Always seeing the best in people.'' He looked back at Dane. ''Whether or not they deserve it.''

Dane wasn't particularly accustomed to feeling sympathy. Particularly toward a cop. And cowboy hat and boots or not, Shane Golightly *was* a cop. A member of the fine law enforcement establishment that didn't give a damn that Alan Michaels was at large. ''The world needs dreamers, too.'' God knew his sister was still one. Amazing, given all she'd been through.

''The world chews up dreamers and spits 'em out,'' Shane said flatly. ''Used and broken. That's not gonna happen to my sister.'' He jammed his hat on his head and strode away.

Dane wondered what dreamer the sheriff had loved and lost. He rubbed his hand around his neck and went back inside. Took a shower. Pulled off the soaked bandage from his forehead. The cut underneath looked like hell, but at least it was finally starting to heal over. Good thing. The supply of bandages

Palmer had given him the day of the accident had run out.

Then he went to the kitchen and started rummaging. Ten minutes later he had a hangover remedy in a small juice glass and he went back to Hadley's room. Fortunately, Hadley had left the door unlocked and it opened easily under his touch.

He stepped inside.

She was sprawled facedown on the bed, and her hair flowed around her shoulders, not entirely obscuring the smooth skin of her back that was visible through that filmy shirt. She looked abandoned in her sleep and he stood there for a long moment absorbing the sight.

Her room wasn't anything like he'd figured it would be.

No ruffles or lace. No sweet innocence.

It was vibrant. Sensual. Full of color and texture. Deep, heady reds on the bed and at the window. Rich, dark woods. And there were books. Stacked everywhere. On the bedside table next to an opened notebook with her handwriting scrawled over the pages. On the dresser. Overflowing the bookshelf built into the wall next to the bathroom they were sharing.

And he was obviously a glutton for punishment. He went over to the bed. Sat down on it beside her and picked up the framed photograph on her nightstand. The entire Golightly family, clustered tightly together and all grinning, looked painfully happy.

It was easy picking out Holly Golightly in the photograph. Hadley looked just like her.

He set down the photograph and picked up the opened notebook. Glanced down at what she'd written and found himself smiling a little. He flipped to the front of the notebook quashing his conscience in favor of intense curiosity.

He paged through, reading bits here and there. She had a definite way with words.

He carefully replaced the notebook on the nightstand and tugged the corner of the soft comforter off her head. "Hey," he murmured. "My little writer. You gonna sleep the day away?"

She groaned, obviously not quite as sound as he'd thought. "Be easier if you'd just shoot me now."

He smoothed her hair away from her shoulders. "This'll help." He nudged her fingers with the glass and she opened her eyes, looking at it with suspicion. "Old family recipe," he assured, amused. "I could tell you what's in it, but then I *would* have to kill you."

She pushed up on an elbow and carefully took the glass from him. Lifted it and sniffed delicately at the contents. "It doesn't have any—"

"Alcohol in it?" He shook his head. "No hair of the dog, I promise."

Her soft brown lashes lowered. "Do you always know what I'm thinking?"

"I'll take the fifth on that. Drink it up, sweetness. All of it. One fell swoop. Trust me. You'll make it through the rest of the day to live and write again."

Her heavy gaze flicked to her nightstand, and a flush stained her cheeks. "Go ahead. Make fun. Everyone else does, too."

"I'm not making fun of you. If you want to be a writer, then write, Hadley. There's nothing that you can't accomplish if you want."

She eyed him, clearly trying to decide if he was serious or not.

"Drink," he ordered softly.

Her lips pressed together. But after a moment she lifted the small glass and drank, making a slight face as she did so. When she was finished, she pressed her lips together. "Tastes sweet. I...thank you."

He ran his thumb over her lower lip, brushing away an imaginary drop of the remedy. She was the sweet one. And he wasn't. He was way too human and she had the softest lips he'd ever touched.

Lips that parted slightly under the graze of his thumb.

And then he felt the tip of her tongue tasting him.

He yanked back his hand like some damn scalded cat.

"Something wrong?" Her eyes had sharpened and the corners of her lips were curling upward.

"Call your dad," he said abruptly. If she ever discovered her own feminine power, she'd be a terror.

She slowly sat up and swung her long legs off the side of the bed. "I already did. He was fine about it. You and Shane are the ones who were upset that I went to the Tipped Barrel. Not even Wendell was put off. He even asked me to go away with him for the weekend."

"You're not going."

Her eyebrows rose. "*That's* why you and Shane always seem so at odds. You're two of a kind. Full of orders." She pushed off her bed. "Maybe I will go with Wendell. He probably won't be so choosy about bedding a dreaded virgin." Her cheeks were pink, her tone defiant.

He snorted. "If the guy was that determined to get you into bed, Hadley, he wouldn't be wasting time trying to show you how to see a freckled owl from a hundred yards."

Her lips compressed, making him want to kiss her all the more until they softened up.

"Bird-watching is important to him."

"And it isn't to you," he countered. "The only thing you two have in common is claiming Lucius as your home town." He didn't know why he kept at it. If she were involved with the other man, she'd be off-limits and he wouldn't be battling this grow-ing…obsession.

And if wishes were horses, beggars would ride.

"What does it matter to you," she asked stiffly. "You and I don't have anything in common, either."

He deliberately closed his hands over her shoulder and felt the fine shimmer ripple through her at the contact. He lowered his head closer to hers. "Does Wendell make you feel that? Does he make you tremble?"

She tossed her head back, her eyes stormy yet still full of some mute appeal that made him ache all the way to his back teeth. "Wendell doesn't say one thing and do another," she whispered huskily.

Which was only the truth, he knew. He was the worst kind of dog. Wanting and not taking yet not wanting anyone else to take, either.

"Virginity is a matter pretty expediently eliminated," she said. "Whether it's with Wendell or someone else."

Anger flooded through him in the split second before common sense prevailed. "There's nothing expedient about it to you. Or you wouldn't still be...chaste." It was an old-fashioned term, yet there was no one who more aptly fit the word.

"So I'm well and truly stuck, aren't I? You don't want to waste your time on someone like me. And the only way for me to not be, well, you know, would be to...to sleep with someone else. Only problem is, I don't want to do that with anyone else." Her lips curved, but there was no humor in it. "Except you. *Maybe,*" she tacked on belatedly.

"It's not a matter of wasting my time." He wanted to shake her for thinking it. "It's a matter of not hurting you." He released her and shoved his hands in his pockets where they couldn't do even more damage.

"I'm a big girl, Wood. You even said so yourself. Don't you think I should be the judge of what might or might not hurt me?"

Trust the bewitching thing to toss his own words back in his face. "I don't get involved with people I care about, okay? They'd just end up getting hurt."

Her eyes went wider. A swallow worked down her long, elegant throat. She crossed her arms over her chest, her hands cupping her elbows, and he dragged his gaze away from the shadowy cleavage beneath that filmy gray.

"Sounds lonely."

Better that she think that than to know the rest of the truth. If she knew the way he'd been lying all this time, she'd never forgive him.

"How's the hangover?" No finesse there. Just a grinding need to change the subject, and her expression softened even more, as if she understood him perfectly.

"My head doesn't feel so awful anymore." She ducked her chin slightly. She traced out a pattern on the carpet with her pink-tipped toe. "You were right. Whatever was in that concoction, it's already helping."

"Good."

She uncrossed her arms again. Tugged at her ear. Displaying every sign of nervousness. "I should apologize to you, too."

"Why?"

"For putting you in such an awkward position. I, um, I won't bother you anymore." She pulled open her bedroom door and smiled a little, even if it didn't reach her eyes. "You're safe from my clutches."

"Hadley—"

"No." She lifted her hand. "Don't say anything. My ego can't take any more humiliation for the day, not even when I'm my own cause of it."

"I'm the one who's sorry, Hadley." More than he could say. "I'll find somewhere else to stay until the car is finished."

"You don't have to go elsewhere," she assured. "You need to come to Evie's party, too. It was your idea in the first place. If nothing else, you'll get plenty of good food and drink. And heaven knows, the invitee list is so large already, one more is not going to harm a single thing. I'm not sure how it's gotten so out of hand. I swear, half the town is coming.''

''Hire some help, then. Bring in servers or something.'' It's what Marlene did for all of the Rutherford parties.

''Hmm. Maybe I will. Anyway, about staying here. You're welcome as long as you need.'' Her fingers were wrapped so tightly around the doorknob her knuckles looked white. But her expression was smooth, and he blamed himself for putting the guarded look in her eyes. ''No charge, of course. It's my fault you're stuck in Lucius, remember?''

He sighed and stepped out into the hall, leaving behind that lush, surprising inner sanctum, and feeling colder as a result. ''I'm not that stuck, sweetness.''

Then he turned and left before he did any more damage than he'd already done.

Chapter Ten

"I'm glad I followed your suggestion," Hadley announced, drawing Wood's attention away from the long table laden with a variety of foods that would have made her mother proud. "You know. Hiring a few waitresses to help out tonight at the party."

It was the first direct statement she'd made to Wood all that week. Ever since she'd made such a fool of herself at the Tipped Barrel, and afterward. It was also the first time that they'd found themselves more or less alone.

Or as alone as two people could be in the presence of at least fifty others.

His head turned as he glanced over at the waitresses who were circling the room with trays of hors d'oeuvres. Mandy Manning was the pretty new girl from the Tipped Barrel, and Bethany Seavers was from the Luscious Lucius. They'd both jumped at the chance to pick up some extra cash, so everyone seemed to be benefiting all the way around.

Wood glanced back at her. "Good. Except, I don't see you not working yourself into exhaustion, so I'm not sure if you've quite got the hang of relying on the ones you hired." He had a plate in his hand, but as far as she could tell, he'd been doing more studying of the food than eating it.

He hadn't taken a single meal at Tiff's in the past several days, either.

She finished dumping her bag of ice into a barrel that held countless bottles of beer and cans of soda. If there were fifty adult guests, there were probably half again as many children racing all around the hall of the church.

"I'm more comfortable having things to keep me busy," she admitted. She lifted the empty bag and crumpled it between her hands. "But this crowd would have been too much for me. I'm just glad to see Evie smiling. I think she was truly surprised."

Wood pulled a beer out of the bucket, apparently losing interest altogether in filling his plate. "Where's Charlie?"

Hadley lifted her shoulder. Her brother-in-law was supposed to have been the one to get Evie to the party. But the task had fallen to Beau when Charlie failed to follow through. "Evie said something about him being out on a job again." She didn't believe it for a minute, though. She knew Stu and Shane hadn't bought it, either. But Evie didn't look as if she were missing him particularly.

And tonight was for celebrating, anyway. Which Evie did seem to be doing. For once.

"Yet Charlie's father is here," Wood murmured.

"Yes." She glanced over where the aging man was seated at a round table. He had a drink in front of him and a plate of food. But he spoke little to anyone else there. "Wonder what he thinks about the fact that his own son—the guest of honor's husband—isn't. He's leaving town again tomorrow. Evie has to drive him back to the airport. I'm watching the kids for her when she goes."

She clamped down on her babbling tongue and picked up a big serving spoon, poking at the candied yams in the silver warming dish and desperately wanting Wood not to wander off again. There had been plenty of people he'd been talking to most of the evening. He didn't seem to have any trouble at all fitting in. He and Shane had even been relatively civil to each other.

"How's *your* father?" she asked.

"The same. He was conscious just long enough to refuse having surgery again." His lips twisted.

"Do you have more siblings besides Darby?"

"No."

"Are you close?"

"Is this twenty questions?" He tilted the bottle to his lips and drank.

Hadley frowned a little. Was he trying to prove his claim of not being a nice guy?

But he lowered the bottle after a moment. "We

used to be close," he said. "When we were kids. She's a strong person though. She doesn't hold on to the…stuff she dealt with during her childhood. She's married. Has a passel of kids." Then he looked over the crowd. "Not many new people come through Lucius."

Her eyebrows drew together at the observation. She'd give anything to understand what made the man tick. "Well, we tend to notice strangers," she allowed. "It's nice here in Lucius. Safe." She smiled as a group of children raced through the room, weaving in and out of the adults. "All these kids can play in their front yards or ride their bikes downtown without their parents having to worry they'll be snatched or something."

Wood's gaze slanted her way again, unreadable and sinfully blue. "Odd choice of words."

Confusion nettled her. "What? Worried?"

"Snatched."

She paused, wishing yet again that she were as adept at reading his thoughts as he seemed to be where she was concerned. "Well, you must know what I mean. Lucius is a pretty safe place, that's all. Not like some cities."

"Hmm." His thumb picked at the label on his bottle. "If I hadn't known your dad was a preacher, I'd have never guessed it. Not many ministers I know who wear Stetsons and drink beer from a bottle."

Hadley smiled, more naturally this time. "He's great, isn't he?" Beau was standing in a circle of friends, his salt-and-pepper head thrown back as he laughed uproariously over some joke. "Shane looks a lot like him. It's no wonder my mother fell for him right off the bat. Love at first sight and all that. Talked about them being fated to meet. But she would have loved him even if it weren't for his name being Golightly. She always said that meeting Beau was the best thing that ever happened to either one of us.''

"Right. You mentioned that he wasn't your natural father. You must have been a baby when they got married, though.''

Hadley nodded, remembering all too vividly what she and Wood had been doing during *that* particular conversation.

Making out in the cab of her truck like a couple of teenagers. Until her virginity had doused it all.

"She and her first husband split up before I was even born. The guy might be biologically responsible for my existence, but Beau's the only father I've ever known. Or wanted. And despite my complaints about them, I ended up with two brothers and a sister whom I dearly love.''

"You were lucky, then. I was right in the center of my parents' divorce.''

Her fingers closed a little too tightly over a fresh bag of homemade rolls. His eyes were dark with memories. "Children often feel that way. But the parents are still the adults, Wood. Even yours. You were a boy. They're the ones responsible. Period.''

"Not in their case.'' His voice was even. But when he tilted the bottle to his lips again and moved away from the table of food, his expression was so solemn that her heart squeezed.

She looked down at the table of food. She could keep hiding behind it, taking care of mindless little chores that she'd already hired Mandy and Bethany to handle, or she could follow after him.

She still hesitated.

The sight of Wendell making his way through the tables toward her spurred her on, and she hurried after Wood, catching up with him near the stairs leading up from the basement hall. "Wood."

He stopped and looked back at her. "Yes?"

He was wearing a black sweater that draped his wide shoulders in a painfully perfect way, and dark khaki pants, and she actually had to take a moment to catch her breath because he was simply so good to look at.

"Do, um, do you want to dance?" It wasn't at *all* what she'd intended to say. And certainly not because she didn't want to dance with him—sober this time. "I hired a live band, but nobody's taking advantage of it and it's getting really late," she hurried on. "Maybe if we got them started…"

"I don't think that's a good idea, Hadley."

"Getting these people away from the tables where they're sitting onto the dance floor, or you dancing with me?" She knew what the answer to that was, though. Apparently she had a masochistic streak inside her as well as wimpiness.

"You did a good thing here tonight, Hadley. Go enjoy it." He started up the steps.

"Stu's getting his cast off next week," she called up after him. "He'll probably be working even faster on your car then." She knew Wood had spent a good deal of time at the garage working on it himself, because Stu had told her so.

He pressed his hand to the wall beside him and looked back at her. "I'm sure he will be. The last of the parts came in this morning."

Stu hadn't told her that, and she hated the way her stomach dropped to her toes at the news. "Well, that's great for you." She kept her tone cheerful even though she feared she might choke on it. "You'll have the sight of Lucius in your rearview mirror before you know it."

"Had." Stu came up behind her, scooping his arm around her waist. "Where you heading off to? Dad's gonna sing in a minute."

Sure enough, Beau had climbed up on the stage and was talking to the guitarist. She looked up at Wood. "Are you going back to Tiff's?"

"I have some calls to make."

He was lying. She knew it with every fiber of her being.

She managed to smile anyway, and let Stu draw her away from the stairs. In minutes the hall was full of music and Beau's rich voice. When she looked again at the staircase, Wood was gone.

Shane dropped his arm over her shoulder and lowered his mouth to her ear. "Put another smile on your face, turnip, or dad's going to know something's wrong."

She blinked back the burning behind her eyes and smiled up at her brother. "You're a pain in the behind, you know that?"

"Yeah," he agreed. "So are you." He dropped a kiss on her head.

Minutes later Beau finished his song and led everyone in a rowdy round of "Happy Birthday" for Evie. And with her sister smiling and her family crowding around her, Hadley managed to tell herself that everything was going to be just fine.

She'd just have to learn how to survive the idea of her life without Wood in it.

It shouldn't be that hard. She'd only known him little more than a week.

Now who was lying?

Dane stood outside the church, his fists shoved in the pockets of his coat. Through the windows near the ground he could see straight down into the hall where the party was going on. Straight down where the Golightlys clustered in a tight, familial group. And maybe Evie was the center of that circle at the moment, but it was Hadley he watched. Hadley dressed in a pale-pink slip of a dress that made her hair look darker and her skin even creamier.

Hadley's family nosed into one another's lives, got angry, got over it. And underneath everything, they were a unit. One that laughed together. Sang together. Hung together in good or bad.

He'd never expected to envy them. But he did.

Sighing, he turned and started walking away from the church, only to stop at the hiss of his name.

His real name.

He looked over. Mandy stood shivering near the

corner of the church building. "What are you doing out here?"

"I've been trying to get your attention for an hour," she said impatiently. Her hands closed over his arm. "You're gonna love this. Michaels was issued a speeding ticket late this afternoon just outside of Billings."

Adrenaline shot through him. He hadn't *really* expected Charlie's father to turn out to be Alan Michaels, but seeing the man in person and knowing he wasn't had been more of a blow than he'd expected. "Outside of Billings. Coming this way or going the other?"

Her lips stretched into a satisfied smile. "This way. And, I've got a license number and vehicle description." She leaned closer to him, her voice low. Excited. "We're gonna find this guy, Dane. We really are." She laughed a little and squeezed his arm tighter.

Nothing ever excited Mandy more than getting a leg up on an investigation.

"Excuse me."

His adrenaline took a header into the snow. Hadley stood on the church steps, the light from the opened doors shining out around her like some halo.

Mandy quickly let go of Dane's arm, but it was too little too late. Hadley had obviously seen, and the conclusion she'd drawn was clear in just those two words.

He walked over to the foot of the steps leading up to the door. "What do you need, Hadley?"

With the light behind her, he couldn't see her expression. "We're cutting the cake." She directed her comment toward Mandy. "Perhaps if you're not too busy out here, Bethany could use your help."

One part of Dane silently took note of the unusual authority in Hadley's voice and applauded her for it.

"Right. Absolutely." Mandy bounded up the stairs past Hadley, giving Dane a quick eyebrows-raised look from behind her.

Hadley didn't step back inside the church doors, however. She continued standing there, looking at Dane. "Mandy's the woman you were with last Sunday night, isn't she. And she's the reason why you seem to have your own bar stool already at the Tipped Barrel. It's not the pool tables that draw you there. You could have just told me, you know. Saved us both some…embarrassment."

"Hadley—"

"Excuse me. My family is waiting for me." She turned on her heel and went inside.

The door—bright red even under the moonlight—closed gently after her.

Dane grabbed the iron rail, started to go up the stairs. To stop her. Tell her the truth. She might hate him for lying, but she wouldn't hate him for thinking he preferred another woman over her.

The cell phone in his pocket vibrated.

Dammit.

He yanked it out, peering at the lighted display.

It was Darby. She hadn't called in several days.

He snapped it to his ear, moving back around to the windows where he could beat himself a little more with the sight of the merry Golightlys inside. ''Yeah?''

''Don't tell me you're in the middle of a business meeting,'' Darby warned in her husky voice. Her vocal cords had been damaged during the kidnapping. ''It's got to be close to eleven o'clock.''

''After,'' he said shortly. ''What's wrong?''

''Dad had another…episode tonight. His surgeon says if he doesn't operate now, there's going to be no point in operating at all.''

Dane rubbed his hand down his face, his nerves tightening. ''Is he conscious?''

''No. Not since the other day. Dane, you have to do this. I know Dad categorically refused surgery. But as long as he's incapacitated, you have his power of attorney, right?''

''For business purposes,'' Dane countered roughly. ''*Not this.*''

''Maybe this wasn't his intention, but you can make it work, Dane. I know you can give permission. The surgeon wants to do it tonight. Even Mother is here. At the hospital. She agrees. We can fax the permission forms to you while they prep Dad for the surgery.''

''And if he dies?'' The question ripped out of his throat. He stared through the window at the Golightlys. A light snow had started falling and it was like looking through some damn kid's snow globe at the perfect family.

''He's going to die for certain without it.'' Darby's voice was low. Pleading. ''Please, Dane. I know this is hard for you. And I know he's said he doesn't want the surgery. But do you really think Daddy wants to *die?*''

Did he? A lifetime of memories congealed into one blurry moment in his head. He exhaled roughly. ''Hold on. I'm gonna have to find you a fax number to use.''

He went back inside the church, down the stairs. The band was playing ''Sweet Home, Alabama'' and Hadley was passing out slices of cake as if her life depended on it.

She hadn't seen him. Just as well.

He went over to Shane. ''I need to have something faxed. Now. Does the church have one?''

Shane shook his head. ''Never needed one.''

''What about your office, then.'' He knew the sheriff office *had* to have a fax.

''What's got your tail in a knot?''

''Yes or no?''

The sheriff's eyes narrowed. But after a moment the sheriff reeled off the phone number, which Dane relayed to Darby.

''The nurse is sending it right now,'' his sister said. ''Are you going to come back tonight?''

Dane eyed the man standing beside him. ''I can't,'' he said gruffly. Roth would want Dane to settle the Alan Michaels business before all else. Even sitting in the hospital waiting room. *Especially* sitting in the hospital. ''I'll explain later.''

''Guess you want to head over to the office and get whatever it is that's so important,'' Shane drawled when Dane snapped the phone shut. He made no secret that helping out "Wood" was not high on his list of priorities.

"I'd appreciate it." Dane kept his own voice even.

The other man slid a look toward his sister who was still occupied. He set his slice of cake on a nearby table. "Let's go, then."

They went up the stairs. Shane's SUV was parked in the no-parking zone. One of the perks of the job. They were at the man's office in minutes.

Shane flipped on the lights and strode across the room. Several pieces of paper were waiting in the tray of the fax machine. He picked them up. Scanned them.

And went still for a long moment. Then he slowly turned and handed them to Dane.

"Well," he murmured, as Dane scrawled his signature on the bottom of the pages. "When I said I didn't believe you were Wood Tolliver, I never expected to find out you were a Rutherford instead. Guess you could buy up every '68 Shelby still in existence if you wanted."

Dane stuck the pages in the machine and punched out the number. The first sheet immediately slid into the fax and he pulled out his phone, dialing Darby. "Form's on its way. Call me when he's in surgery." Then he hung up again and faced the sheriff.

"That form's for your father." Shane was looking at the machine. "There was an article in the paper just this morning about Roth Rutherford still being in the hospital."

"And if word got out that I'm in Lucius, that

would be in the newspaper, too,'' Dane said evenly. ''And I don't want that.''

He was surprised when the sheriff didn't question his reasons. ''My sister's in love with you,'' he said flatly. ''Or mighty close to it, given the fact you've only had a week so far to mess with her head.''

''Believe me. She's been messing with mine.'' Dane's hands curled.

''You need to go back where you come from, Mr. Rutherford.'' There wasn't one ounce of deference in Shane's voice. If anything, his anger was colder than ever. ''You've done all the damage here you're gonna do.''

''I never wanted to hurt Hadley,'' Dane said, his voice low. Tight. ''She's the best—'' He broke off. He wasn't going to bare his thoughts to the sheriff. Not on this day or any other. ''And I'll go when I'm ready. Unless you want to lock me up again for…what kind of charge do you want to make up?''

Shane looked furious. ''Believe me. If I could come up with something that might stick long enough to break up whatever hold you've got going with Hadley, I'd put you in a cell in a stone-cold minute.''

And Dane's attorney would make certain that Sheriff Shane Golightly never found another day's work in law enforcement. Yet warning the other man of that held no appeal.

''Thanks for the use of the fax,'' he said instead, and plucked the finished document out of the tray. He folded it in thirds, shoved it in the inner pocket of his jacket and walked out of the office, the bell over the door jangling.

Dane went back to Tiff's. The place was empty because everyone was still at Evie's birthday party. He went into the parlor where there was a tasteful display of liquor bottles behind the leaded glass doors of an antique breakfront.

He opened one of the doors and pulled out the bottle of scotch.

Then he went to his room and waited for Darby to call.

Hadley tied off the last bulging trash bag and handed it to Stu to carry out to the trash before pulling on her coat. "Where'd Shane disappear to?"

Stu shrugged. He waited until Hadley was heading up the stairs before flipping off the lights. They were the last stragglers to depart. Beau had already left to drive Evie and the children home.

"Saw you dancing with Wendell," Stu commented.

"Don't sound so satisfied. I told Wendell that he should find another person more suited to him."

"Why?"

"Because I'm never going to love him, that's why." *Because I know what love feels like now.* And a broken heart. She pushed open the main doors of the church and waited for him to exit before locking it up behind them. Even if Wood hadn't burst into her life, she wouldn't love Wendell Pierce.

It was snowing again. Just a gentle drift of flakes. "Would you go around with some woman who had expectations of you that you knew were never going to come to pass? Of course not,'' she answered for him. ''It would be cruel.''

He just grunted a little and took the trash around to the bin at the rear of the church. She waited in her truck until he came back around. But instead of going to his own SUV, he walked over to her. She rolled down her window. ''Forget something?''

''It was a good party. I'm glad you thought of it.''

''It was Wood's idea, actually.'' The admission made her ache. She leaned out the window and kissed his cheek. ''I love you, Stu. You're a good brother, even if you do make me crazy.'' Then she started the engine.

Looking somewhat surprised, he stepped back, and she rolled up the window and drove home. The house was silent and dark when she arrived. She carried in the various empty containers she'd used for some of the food and stacked them on the kitchen counter. She'd already washed them in the church kitchen, and for a moment she wished she hadn't. Then she could have busied herself with one more task before going to her bedroom.

She didn't know if Wood would be in his room, or if he'd be alone, or if he'd have the lovely Mandy Manning at his side yet again.

Sometimes ignorance really was bliss.

She shoved the containers in the cupboard with a little more force than necessary.

Well, maybe not bliss. But certainly less painful than having one's worst suspicion borne out.

But she could only put off the inevitable for so

long. And it was well after midnight. She'd promised to watch Evie's kids again the next day.

She mentally stiffened her spine and walked down the hall to her bedroom.

Wood's door was closed. A thin line of light shined from beneath it.

She quickened her step and went inside her room, closing the door firmly behind her. Her heart was pounding inside her chest and she leaned back against the door. But closing her eyes just made her see the branded image of Wood and Mandy jumping apart like two guilty lovers.

Opening her eyes again, she stared at her room. It was the only space inside Tiff's that felt really hers. She'd decorated it to suit only herself. The rest of the place was still a monument to her mother.

She found no comfort in her room tonight, though. Not among her beautiful colors or her stacks of books or her neatly organized notebooks where she penned her stories and dreamed of one day seeing her name on the cover of a book.

"Lord, Hadley. You're depressing yourself," she whispered aloud.

She straightened from the door and hung up her coat, and changed out of her party dress and into her pajamas. She added the dress to the bag for the dry cleaners. Her pink coat with Wood's bloodstains on it was still in the bag. She'd been so busy she hadn't managed to get it to the cleaners yet. The stain was probably so set in by now it would never come out.

She yanked the drawstring closed on the bag and

shoved it back in the corner of her closet and went into the bathroom, only to stop short.

The connecting door to Wood's bedroom was still open.

She quietly padded over to it, intending only to quickly pull it closed. She wasn't going to look in his room. She wasn't.

Her eyes had other ideas.

She looked in the room. The light that she'd seen beneath his door came from a single lamp on the nightstand. He was sitting, fully dressed on the bed, a bottle in one hand, a glass in the other.

Her stomach felt as if it would never be free of the knot in which it had tied itself. And even though she knew she was the biggest fool to ever walk the planet, she stepped into the doorway.

And had an unbidden memory of the day she'd gone to see him at Shane's office. When he'd been in the cell.

"Wood? Are…are you all right?"

His head slowly turned and he looked at her. And though the light wasn't overly bright, she could see the pain in his eyes.

The expression on his face made her ache. Maybe there were no physical bars caging him tonight. But there were definitely emotional ones.

And she wished with everything she was that she were the one who could give him the key.

She forgot that she was wearing her oldest pair of pajamas. That she was not the woman he wanted.

She stepped into his room. "What's wrong?"

His head tipped back against the headboard behind him. "Do you believe in forgiveness, Hadley?"

She swallowed. Took a few steps closer to the side of the bed. She recognized the bottle of scotch. She'd bought it to have on hand for Shane when he came for Christmas day dinner. "Yes, I do."

A muscle in his jaw flexed. "I don't."

The level of alcohol in the bottle had barely gone down. And there was a narrow amount still in the glass. "Then going through life must be really difficult," she murmured. "Who is it that you don't want to forgive?"

"Don't want to. Can't." His lips twisted. "Is there a difference? I'm not sleeping with Mandy Manning."

Her breath escaped on a harsh puff. "There's *something* between the two of you."

"She's an old friend of mine," he said after a moment.

"One you just happened to run into in the thriving metropolis of Lucius, Montana? I may not be as...worldly...as you'd prefer, but I'm not stupid, Wood."

He leaned over and carefully placed the glass and bottle on his nightstand. "No. You're not stupid." He came off the bed like some uncoiling, dangerous animal. "You're decent and creative and beautiful. Inside. Outside. You put everyone else before yourself, and *you* believe in forgiveness."

She looked up into his face, feeling surrounded by him. "What's happened? What's wrong? Is it your father?"

His eyes narrowed down to slits. His fingers threaded through her hair, grazing her shoulder through the blue-and-white striped cotton of her pajama top. ''He's in surgery,'' he said after a moment. ''And I'm the one who put him there.''

She couldn't prevent her hands from lifting. Pressing against his chest covered in that fine, thin black cashmere. She could feel the hard beat of his heart and felt her own trip unevenly before settling into the same tempo. ''Wanting to make your father better is nothing that needs forgiveness, Wood. Wasn't his need for surgery what you and he disagreed over?''

''The latest thing.'' He fingered the pointed collar of her top. Flattened it out over her shoulder blade. ''The disagreements for us go back a lot further than that.''

She swallowed. Her skin felt prickly. Sensitive. Tight. One part of her mind was dimly aware of her fingertips bunching into the softness of his shirt, feeling the hardness beneath.

''Families disagree,'' she said faintly. ''Look at mine. We're always—''

''I did look.'' His gaze worked down her face. ''I have…advantages, Hadley. A lot of them. More than anybody should have a right to. But I've never had what you've got with your family. Or maybe I did a long time ago. Before I screwed things up so badly my entire family fell apart.''

Her eyes suddenly burned. ''It can't have been that bad.''

His lashes lifted. And the memories writhing in

his blue, blue gaze tore at her. He sighed raggedly, thumbing away a tear that snuck out of her eye. His palm ran down her head. Tangled gently in her hair. "Are you sure you believe in forgiveness?"

"Yes," she whispered.

"Then will you forgive me for this?"

Her lips parted.

Her head fell back as his mouth covered hers.

Chapter Eleven

Hadley inhaled the taste of him. Her fingers clutched his sweater, balling it against her sensitive palms. "Wood."

"Shh." His mouth burned along her jaw. Found her ear. "Don't talk."

Since she could barely form a coherent thought, it was probably a good thing. She jerked, gasping, when his teeth gently found her earlobe, followed by the flick of his tongue.

Heat streaked through her, pooling inside her. She craned her head around, mutely finding his mouth again with hers, impossibly greedy for more. Always more.

And he gave.

His hands inched their way down her spine.

Slowly walked the cotton up between his fingers until they touched her bare skin. She trembled wildly and arched against his palm. Her hands slid down, shoving under his sweater. Curling in frustration when she found another shirt beneath it. He exhaled roughly when she yanked at that one as well and pulled it loose.

Then she delved beneath that. And was vaguely shocked at the satisfied sound that purred out of her when she finally pressed her palms against his warm body.

Her fingertips scraped lightly through the whorls of soft hair. But even that wasn't enough.

Only, she was stymied by the buttons. The cashmere over it. She wanted them gone; didn't want to take her hands away for fear this moment would all be just one more tormenting dream. "Your shirt," she mumbled against his lips, finally desperate enough to take a chance. She tugged at the shirt. The sweater. "Please…"

He pulled his hands away from her long enough to yank the sweater over his head. Without wasting time on buttons, the shirt followed and she heard the soft scatter of buttons as several ripped free. Then he grabbed Hadley's wrists and pressed her palms flat against his chest. "Touch me," he muttered.

So many sensations. His body so close to hers. The hard muscles beneath her eager hands. Her own flesh reveling under his touch.

She sifted her fingers through his chest hair, slowly trailing downward, traveling that captivating, narrowing arrow over his hard, sculpted abdomen.

His muscles jumped, his hands tightening for a moment on her waist. He sucked in a hard breath. Pressed his forehead to hers, and she felt exultant.

"Touch *me*," she whispered.

His hands ran up her arms. Kneaded her shoulders. Found the buttons of her pajama top. She sank her teeth into her tongue as she felt him slowly, deliberately unfasten each one, as careful with her as he'd been careless with his own. By the time her top hung loose, her skin felt on fire.

His palms slowly slid beneath the fabric. Drifted over her abdomen. Trailed along her waist, setting off shivering flames along the way.

She flattened her palms, stroking upward. Felt the hard push of his masculine nipples against her palms and felt her own tighten even more in response. "*Touch* me," she whispered again, and stepped closer to him. Until she felt the heat of him even more clearly.

"Here?" His hands finally slid upward, brushing the undersides of her breasts.

She dragged in a needy breath. "Yes."

"Here?" His fingers grazed the outer curves. He lowered his head and pressed his mouth to the base of her neck.

Sensations cramped through her. Her knees turned weak and she grabbed his shoulders. His hair brushed her chin and she turned her head, rubbing her cheek against those rich, chestnut strands. "Yes."

He made a low sound and slid an arm around her waist, hauling her up onto her toes. Beyond. His mouth burned down the valley between her breasts.

The sound of his harsh breathing was a symphony in her ears. And then his mouth covered her breast.

She shuddered from the inside out and was barely aware of him carrying her the few feet to the bed. He set her carefully on her feet and she whimpered, wanting his mouth on her again. Her arms twined around his neck and he leaned over her, taking her easily with him as he yanked back the quilt, dislodging the pillows with abandon.

Then the bed was beneath her and his chest was pressing against hers and her legs were tangling with his, and oh, she wished there weren't still so many clothes between them.

He kissed her again, seeming once more to read her mind as he pushed the top off her shoulders and cupped her breasts again. His thumbs dragged over her tight nipples, again and again and again until her nerves were tight as wires. His hair was thick, silky as her fingers twined through it. Their tongues danced.

And her heart still cried for more.

She ran her hands down the hot silk of his back. Tugged at the confines of his belt. His pants.

He reared back, grabbing her hands tightly in his. His chest heaved with his breathing. His gaze burned into her. "Are you sure?"

She wasn't sure about anything except that she might die if he pulled away from her now. "Yes." She twined her leg over his. "I want you."

His jaw tightened for a moment, and her heart simply stopped, hovering there on the precipice, willing him to come back to her. "I want you," she whispered again. "I want you, I want you—"

His mouth covered hers, swallowing her needful chant. He rolled, pulling her over him until her legs fell to either side of him. Her head pressed into the curve of his neck. His hands were strong, gentle, inexorable when they shaped her hips, pressing her against him. Blinding her with the possibilities. The reality.

She bit her lip, stifling a moan. She would fly apart if his hands didn't hold her together. His fingers flexed. Despite the layers still separating them, she could feel him. That part of him that she could hold inside her for just a little while, even if she couldn't hold *him.*

And then holding back the sounds rising in her throat was impossible, for his long fingers had found the tie at the waist of her pajamas, and he was drawing it loose. The soft, aging cotton gaped and his fingers delved beneath it. His knuckles brushed her abdomen, his fingertips breaching the down between her thighs. Then they dipped even further.

She shuddered wildly, and he made a sound of such deep satisfaction that she wanted to laugh. Cry. Instead she pressed her open mouth against his neck, tasting the warmth of him, the corded tendons. He rolled again, pressing her back against the soft mattress. His mouth covered hers. His thigh was heavy over hers. And his hand, oh, his hand was the most gentle thing she'd ever felt as it covered her.

Her arms twined around him. She could no more

have kept from moving against his hand than she could have flown to the stars.

"Sweetness." His voice was low, a rough growl over her excruciatingly sensitized nerve endings. His fingers swirled. Delved. Pressed. "So sweet. I want all of it. All of you, Hadley. All."

She cried out, convulsing against him.

His mouth covered hers, and the pleasure just went on, and on. And when her shudders finally slowed, when she barely had enough strength left to open her eyes and look into his beautiful, masculine face, his hands finally slid away from her. The bed rocked a little as he rose. Unbuckled his belt. Undressed.

She inhaled slowly, loving the sight of him.

Loving him.

Then he drew her loosened pajama pants down her legs and dropped them on the floor. His hands circled her ankles. Slowly inched their way up her calves. He kissed her knee. The tender skin inside.

She shifted, urgency so quickly renewing itself, engulfing her. She grasped his shoulders, pulling.

"Don't rush me," he warned softly, and pressed another kiss to her leg.

She groaned. But he continued seducing her senses, stealing her soul, as his kisses slowly worked their way up. But when he kissed the point of her hipbone, when his tongue flicked tantalizingly against her navel, she bucked against him, shoving him onto his back.

"Two can play that game," she whispered, and pressed her lips against his chest. Caught a rigid little nipple between her teeth and slid her tongue across it.

He laughed a little, groaned a lot, and tangling his hands in her hair, he hauled her up to his mouth again. "No games," he muttered, and pulled her beneath him once more. His thigh wedged between hers. "I don't want to hurt you."

And this time she knew he was not referring to her emotions. She drew her hands down the wide sweep of his back. "You'll only hurt me if you stop."

He shifted suddenly, sinking into the cradle of her hips. She gasped, nearly coming off the bed so deep was the pleasure, and her movement only pressed her that much closer to him. Her legs moved restively and he slid his hand over her knee in a soothing motion that didn't soothe at all.

"Please…" A tear burned its way down her cheek. "Please just love—"

He kissed her. "Forgive me," he whispered, and slowly sank inside her. He caught her hands in his, fingers tangling. She cried out. Not with pain, but pleasure.

When she realized he was trembling, shuddering, too, she dragged open her heavy lids and looked up at him. He'd frozen, his weight on his arms, their entwined fingers.

She worked her fingers free from his grip. Grazed her fingertip along his eyebrow, over the small scars around his eye. Trailed the slashing line in his hard cheek. Touched the muscle flexing fiercely in his jaw. Laid her palm tenderly against his cheek.

His eyes drifted closed for a moment.

And in that moment she knew that there would never be a time to regret this. No matter what happened, where he went, she'd always love him.

She lifted her head and gently brushed her lips against his. "It's okay," she murmured.

His mouth parted. The bunched muscles in his arms, his shoulders, flexed.

She slid her lips over his again. So soft for a man who was so hard. "Everything will be okay." She caressed his shoulders. Let her hand drift over his shoulder blade. Graze the indentation of his spine. "I won't hurt you."

His lips moved at that. Stretching into a faint smile as she'd wanted. He lowered himself to his elbows, his hands surrounding her head. His gaze burned over her face, as intimate as his body that was seared into hers. Then he murmured her name.

Just that.

Her throat tightened. Her eyes flooded.

He made a soft sound, and he slowly rocked against her.

Pleasure streaked through her. She drew her knees up, urgently hugging his hard, narrow hips.

He shuddered. Thrust harder. Deeper. "Condom's still in my wallet," he said, his voice raw.

"I don't care." How quickly the coin could turn from tenderness to mindless greed. She scrabbled at his hips, pulling him ever closer to her. Everything inside her coiled tighter. Gathered him with her.

"I care." He pushed himself back up on his arms, every tendon in him seeming to stand out in harsh relief. "I won't take chances with you. Not with you."

Despite his words, he bucked hard into her, making her cry out, the pleasure dissolving her from the insides out.

"Hadley." His plea was low, gritting. "Ah, sweetness, you're killing me."

But she was beyond hearing. She could feel him in her heart. Her very soul. And when her body exploded, she thought faintly that she'd been wrong.

She could fly to the stars after all.

She was still spinning in the cosmos when Wood's hands pinned her hips to the mattress as he yanked himself from her, only to sink back against her with a long, low groan, his hot pleasure jetting over her abdomen, and it was so erotic that she writhed wildly against him and flew even higher.

And then the room was silent save the sounds of their ragged breathing.

After a long, stunned while, though, Wood started to shift. "Gotta get a washcloth," he muttered thickly.

Hadley just curled her fingers through his hair where his head pressed against her breast. "Don't move. You're perfect," she whispered. "Stay right here with me. Sleep."

A mammoth sigh shuddered through him.

He stayed with her.

The chilly gray of dawn was creeping into the room when Dane's cell phone softly buzzed. His eyes opened, and he found Hadley looking at him, her eyes blurry with sleep.

She sat up a little, pressing her hand to her tumbled hair, clutching the quilt to her breasts.

He reached out and grabbed the phone off the nightstand and was barely conscious of the prayer that whispered through his mind when he flipped it open. "Darby?"

"Dad made it. We'll know more after the next twenty-four to forty-eight hours."

Dane sank back into the pillows. He hadn't killed off his father. The relief was legions deep. But along with relief was responsibility and priority.

He ran his hand down Hadley's satin smooth spine, and felt something rock solid and angry inside him shift.

"Dane?" Darby's voice prompted him. "You still there?"

His sister had moved on from the kidnapping, why wouldn't he? He stroked Hadley's back again, sank his fingers into her rich, soft hair. Her lips softened even more. "I'll be there," he told his sister.

She was quiet for a moment. "You...will?"

"Yeah." Alan Michaels was still out there somewhere. But Dane was finally realizing that finding the man wasn't going to heal the Rutherford family.

That had to start from the inside. And he'd realized it because of Hadley. Because of her heart. Her generosity. Her family.

"Well. Good." Darby sounded pleased. "Okay, then. I'll call if anything crops up." She hung up, and he slowly folded the phone and set it back on the nightstand.

"Your father?"

He looked at Hadley. "He survived the surgery."

Her head tilted, her eyes soft. "I'm so glad."

They weren't meaningless, polite words to her, either. She meant it.

"I have to go back," he said quietly.

Her eyes tightened a little. But she gave him a soft smile. Nodded her encouragement. "Of course. You should be there."

If he stayed in bed with her, he was going to make love to her again. He looped his hand around her neck and pulled her closer. There were too many words damming up in his throat, and none of them held any concrete form. So he caught her lips in a kiss that lingered longer than he'd intended.

She looked a little dazed when he finally set her from him and climbed out of bed. Dazed or not, her gaze still followed him, and he felt himself hardening.

Her lips parted a little, her eyes going heavy.

"Witch," he murmured, and went into the bathroom before he fell to temptation.

He yanked the shower curtain around the tub, flipped on the water and stepped under the spray before it was even close to getting hot. He had to force himself not to call her name. To bring her beneath the spray of water with him. To lift her legs around his waist and find heaven all over again.

To hold her there for the next decade or two.

He still found himself standing there longer than

necessary, some rusty part of himself hopefully wishing that she'd pull back the curtain of her own accord and join him, whether invited or not.

But she didn't.

And eventually he turned off the water and grabbed a towel. Dashed it over his head. His chest. Wrapped it around his waist.

He looked at his reflection in the mirror above the sink. He rubbed his bristled jaw. He'd probably marred Hadley's skin with it but good.

His body stirred yet again. More insistently.

If he made love to her for the next fifty years would he finally have enough?

He turned away from the reflection. "Hadley. There's something I need to tell you."

She didn't answer, and he walked out of the bathroom. But she wasn't sleeping again. She was sitting on the side of the bed, her long sleek legs bared by the shirt—his white shirt—that he'd worn under his sweater the night before.

And damn, but he liked the sight of her wearing nothing but his shirt. Liked the sight of her sensibly sexy pajamas tangled on the floor with his pants. He nearly pulled the towel loose to see how well she liked it as well. But he didn't. "I need to tell you something."

Her eyes slowly lifted to his, and he realized she was holding his wallet in her hands.

And everything inside him went still.

Cold.

She lifted the opened wallet, like some dreadful offering. "I was going to join you in the shower. I wanted to…before you left Lucius. Me. And I didn't want you to worry about me. So I was going to get—''

''Hadley—''

''—your condom.''

''I can explain.'' But could he? The years of anger. Of carrying his worst failure in his mind, his heart, wherever he went, always with him no matter what he did.

The only time he'd ever truly put it aside was when he was buried so deeply inside her that his world felt right once more.

Her jaw worked. Her lips pressed together. ''You had your driver's license all along. Has my brother known it all along, too?''

''No.'' Dane crossed to her, but she held up her palms. Her eyes were a tangle of warning, and he stopped, hating himself for putting that expression there. ''Not until last night when Darby faxed me the forms for my father's surgery.''

She slowly folded the wallet, closing over the license inside that clearly identified him.

Dane Rutherford of Louisville, Kentucky.

Thirty-seven, six-two, brown hair, blue eyes.

He knew what it should have really said—lying son of a bitch.

She leaned forward and placed the wallet on the nightstand with inordinate care. The lapels of his shirt fell open, exposing the creamy curves of one pink-tipped breast.

''What a stroke of luck for you that I pulled out in front of you on the highway last week,'' she murmured. She straightened again, and his shirt settled into a smooth line over her once more.

His eyes narrowed. "Luck. Fate. Call it what you want, Hadley. I was going to tell you—"

"When?" Her lips stretched into a pained smile.

"This morning. Just now."

She didn't believe him. "Shane warned me. But I wouldn't listen. I was so certain that I knew the true you." She pushed herself off the bed, looking as if she might shatter if she moved too quickly.

"You did know me."

Her lips twisted. "I should have known better. Suspected. I mean, what's a guy like you want with a tiny place like Lucius? With the people who make it their home? Doesn't matter what your name is. Wood. Dane. Talk about a pushover. I just really made your job easy for you, didn't I."

"Job? There's nothing about you that's a pushover." He closed his hands over her shoulders.

And felt her flinch.

He let her go as if she'd burned him, and curled his hands into fists. "Dammit, Hadley, I *was* going to tell you. But there are things you don't know. Things I thought I had to do. Had to make right."

"I understand perfectly," she said. "All these years of being so careful. I thought—" She shook her head. "None of it matters anymore, does it."

"Everything about you matters."

"Nice words. I could almost believe you mean them. If I didn't know the truth about you now." She tilted back her head and looked him right in the face. "Well, congratulations, Dane Rutherford. You were right.'' Her voice went hoarse. ''Some things don't get forgiven.''

''Hadley—''

''I want you to leave.'' She walked through the bathroom and quietly shut the door on her side.

The sound of the lock being turned was as loud as a gunshot to his soul.

Chapter Twelve

The jet touched down on the highway outside of Lucius and slowly taxied to a stop. The little-traveled road had been cordoned off for safety's sake, but the sleek plane with the logo of Rutherford Industries emblazoned on its side had still drawn a fair share of attention from folks who'd driven out of the town limits to see why the highway was being closed off.

Dane climbed out of the sheriff's SUV where he'd been waiting and stood on the cold, wind-blown blacktop. Hadley's brother hadn't assisted with the arrangements to bring the plane in out of any courtesy.

He just wanted to see the back of Dane as rapidly as possible.

Still Dane hesitated, his hand closed over the cold

frame of the passenger door. He wasn't a man who often apologized. "I'm sorry."

Shane's dark sunglasses hid his expression. "Hope that revenge of yours chokes you, Rutherford."

He absorbed that. "Maybe if I'd succeeded, it would have."

"Cut the crap. You came here and got exactly what you wanted."

"Not even close, Sheriff," he assured grimly. "Seems I'm no better at finding justice where the man who kidnapped my sister is concerned than anyone else was."

He shoved the door closed and started toward the plane. The side door opened, and the steps slowly extended. He could see his pilot, Lou Riggs, standing at the top of them and lifted a hand in acknowledgment.

But a hard hand closed over his shoulder and jerked him around. He eyed the sheriff. "What…?" Staying in Lucius—knowing that he'd been responsible for hurting Hadley—was growing more intolerable by the minute.

"Explain."

Dane gave the other man a long look. Orders had never sat well with Dane. He was too used to giving them.

The sheriff sighed mightily and yanked off his sunglasses. He stood nose to nose with Dane. "I'm *asking,*" he said tightly.

"For what? An answer to why the man who kidnapped my sister wasn't put in jail to rot where he belonged? An answer to why two weeks ago he strolled out of the institution where he'd been held all these years and nobody thought to stop him? An answer to why in hell the man was fascinated by this bump in the road of a town while he *was* institutionalized?'' His voice rose. "If I *had* any of those answers, maybe I'd finally be able to live with myself! And why the hell do you care, anyway?''

At the end of his rope, he turned on his heel and strode toward the plane. The phone in his pocket vibrated. But the anger inside him had a vicious appetite, not caring who he took it out on.

And since the caller was probably Darby, he ignored it.

He strode up the steps to the plane and nodded curtly at Lou. "Let's go.''

"Sure thing, Mr. Rutherford.''

Dane took his usual seat. Several newspapers were folded in a stack on the glass table next to it, along with a porcelain pot of coffee that he knew would be steaming hot and perfectly brewed. The glass holding the fresh-squeezed orange juice was cut crystal. The tray bearing an array of croissants, glistening frozen grapes and sliced strawberries matched it.

He knew if he'd expressed a preference for mangos grown in the Caribbean, his staff would have made sure he had them.

The engines were being powered up. Dane closed his eyes.

But all he saw was Hadley's face. He'd known her barely more than a week, and he would never get that look out of his memory.

He opened his eyes.

And swept his arm over the table, sending its contents smashing into the wall.

"Sir?"

He watched the orange juice dripping down the wall to the plush ivory carpet. "Yes, Vivian?"

The flight attendant whose sole responsibility it was to make certain none of the privileged few who boarded Dane's private jet wanted for anything, hesitantly stepped over to him. "There is a call for you."

Her eyes drifted to the mess, and he could only imagine her thoughts. That the ever-controlled boss had well and truly lost it.

"Shall I bring you a phone?" She was obviously nervous but doing an admirable job of hiding it.

He pinched the bridge of his nose. His head ached. Inside and out, where the cut on his forehead throbbed mockingly. "Yes," he sighed. "Thank you."

She nodded quickly and disappeared to the front of the plane, returning a moment later with a cordless unit. He took it from her. "That'll be all."

She quickly made herself scarce, closing the door to the forward cabin behind her. He held the phone in his hand, quelling the desire to send it the way of the croissants and coffee.

The plane turned on a dime and halted while the engines gathered force. He'd be in Louisville before noon.

He lifted the phone to his ear. "Rutherford."

"Where the hell are you going?" Mandy's voice was tart, a testament to their long friendship. "I've been calling your cell, and Tiff's. I finally called Laura and she said you'd summoned the plane.''

"Roth had surgery last night. I'm going back.''

"Oh." She sounded slightly mollified. "Well, you might want to wait on that. I'm in Miles City. Michaels rented a motel room here last night.''

Dane wondered what was taking Lou so long to take off. The engines were screaming. "Handle it, Mandy. You used to be a bounty hunter. If you know where the guy is, take him in. Institution or prison, he's got no right being on the loose.''

"I've already talked to the manager of the motel. Michaels is already gone. He asked for directions of getting to Lucius without using any main roads. Think you might want to handle this one yourself, Dane. You know that ex-wife of Michaels? Hannah? Turns out her full name was Hannah Olivia Leigh.''

"So?"

"She called herself Holly, apparently.''

Dane's world narrowed to a pinpoint.

He threw the phone aside and strode to the front of the plane, throwing open the door to the forward cabin. Vivian gave him a startled look. "Open the passenger door,'' he told her flatly.

Lou and Jeremy Johnson, the new copilot, were staring out the front window. "I'm sorry, sir,'' Lou said apologetically. "I just can't get this bird off the ground as long as that guy won't move his SUV.''

Shane Golightly was blocking the highway.

"It's okay, Lou." He turned back where Vivian had pulled open the heavy door. She started to turn the lever for the stairs and he shook his head, jumping out.

The landing was still jarring through him when he was running toward the SUV. He went to the driver's side and yanked open the door. "Hadley is Alan Michaels's daughter."

Shane didn't answer, but he didn't need to.

Because it finally all made sense to Dane.

"I did not know," he gritted. "Goddamnit, Shane! There were two things Alan Michaels showed an obsession for while he was supposed to be locked away. My sister. Your town. Now are you going to help me find him before he finds the daughter nobody ever wanted him to know about or am I going to do it myself?"

"There's no way he could have found out about Hadley. Holly didn't have her until she'd been living in Lucius for months. She gave up everything she ever knew to get away from that man."

"And that man kidnapped my sister, thinking he'd finally get past being a two-bit nobody by miraculously rescuing her days later, so he could win back the wife who'd left him. The guy is a freakin' bastard and he's on his way to Lucius."

"You led him here."

"I *followed* him here. Jesus Christ, Golightly. You think I want anyone else to be hurt by him? Especially Hadley? I'm in love with her, and I don't love anybody." Even as the words came out, Dane knew they were the truest words he'd spoken since he'd taken on Wood Tolliver's name.

Shane exhaled. "Get in."

Dane went around and climbed in. Shane wheeled the vehicle around and headed toward town. "And do something about getting that plane off my highway."

Dane pulled out his cell and called the plane. He didn't even look back to make sure his instructions were followed. The SUV flew past the turnoff to the abandoned skating rink. Shane had turned on his flashers but not the siren.

"Hadley is supposed to be watching Evie's kids this morning," Shane murmured. "If Michaels does get to Lucius and he does find Tiff's, at least Hadley won't be there."

Dane stared out the windshield. "Drive faster."

Hadley added a last piece of wood to her armload and carried it inside, dumping the split logs into the bin in the kitchen. Her body ached from the inside out, but it was nothing compared to the hollow ache inside her chest.

Wood—no, it was *Dane*—was gone.

She'd told him to go, and he had.

If only she could order her heart around so surely.

She hung her flannel coat on the hook by the door and went into the dining room, picking up the rest of the dishes left from breakfast and carrying them to the kitchen.

The house was painfully silent. No laborious piano playing from Mrs. Ardelle. No clink of a cereal bowl from Joanie. She'd gone with Mrs. Ardelle into Billings to bargain shop for the baby.

At breakfast they'd even talked about the possibility of sharing an apartment. Mrs. Ardelle could watch Joanie's baby once it arrived, and Joanie could still work and finish school. Even Vince had gone out after putting away his fair share of eggs and muffins.

She poured herself a cup of coffee and sat at the counter, staring into it but not drinking.

It had only been a week. How could she lose her heart to a man after only a week?

She lowered her forehead to her hand and blinked back the tears. She'd done enough crying locked in her bedroom at dawn. Until she'd heard the movements in Wood—*Dane's* room cease.

Until she'd felt the complete absence of his presence in her boardinghouse. An aging Victorian that was home to half a dozen people, and still felt empty.

She sucked in a harsh breath. Sitting there crying over him wasn't going to make anything better. She shouldn't have canceled watching Evie's kids. At least she'd have been *busy.*

She slid off the stool, carrying her coffee. But before she could head down the hall to her bedroom the front door opened.

Her fingers tightened. But it wasn't Dane.

Of course it wasn't Dane.

She'd told him to go. And he had.

This man was no taller than she was. His hair was gray and sparse, his face lined.

You take in strays. Dane's statement whispered through her mind and she banished it. "Can I help you?"

He stared at her for a moment. Then he smiled a little. "You haven't changed at all."

"I'm sorry?"

He pushed the door closed behind him and took a few steps toward her. "I've been looking for years. Why did you run?"

Her stomach dipped. She tightened her grip on her coffee mug. "Do I know you?"

His steps faltered. "Don't. Don't do that. You know it bothers me."

How many times had Evie lectured her about leaving the door open for anyone and their mother's brother to walk in? "I didn't mean to bother you," she said carefully. "I'm afraid I'm out of rooms to rent, if you're looking for a place to stay. But the Lucius Inn on the other side of town probably has vacancies."

"You'd make me stay in a different place?" His brows drew together. "Darling, you can't mean that. I've come so far."

Her feet slowly slid back. She was even with the kitchen doorway. "How far?"

He frowned. "You know how far."

"Of course. Silly me." She backed up another step. But he followed. Her heart was in her throat. "You're, um, you're looking fine."

He paused at that. Brushed his hand over his hair in a self-conscious gesture. "I've gotten old. But you haven't. You're just the same as always, Hannah. So lovely."

Her fingers went lax, and the coffee mug seemed to fall in slow motion to the linoleum floor that her mother had maintained all the years of Hadley's childhood.

Her mother. Whom nobody had ever called Hannah.

The mug crashed and splintered. Hot coffee splattered over her stockinged feet, burning through to her skin.

He closed the distance between them. "Don't move, darling. You'll cut yourself."

Hadley swallowed. "Yes, Alan," she whispered. For that was the only person he could possibly be. The one person whom Holly Golightly had ever truly feared. The person whom everyone—Beau, Evie, Stu, Shane, Hadley—had been warned to always guard against.

Her natural father.

He smiled beatifically.

His eyes were dark brown. Like hers.

"That's my darling, Hannah."

Dane stood on the other side of the rear door, listening to the murmured voices coming from inside. Hadley's brother was at the front of the house, prepared to go in that way. They had no way of knowing what they'd find...if the guy—who'd parked his aging sedan in front of God and country right at the curb on the street—was armed. Or *what* he planned.

But when Dane heard the smash of glass, he closed his hand over the doorknob, chancing a look through the window.

And he had his first sight since he was sixteen years old, of Alan Michaels, in the flesh.

In that moment it was all he could do not to smash through the door and go for the man's throat for the thing he'd done to Darby.

Hadley stood in the midst of broken crockery. Dark liquid—coffee—was pooled around her on the floor. And as Dane stood there struggling with a deep need to do harm, Michaels knelt and carefully plucked the pieces of broken mug from around Hadley's feet.

How many reports had Dane read about the man? How many photographs, accounts, had he seen?

He pushed open the door and stepped into the kitchen.

Hadley jerked, turning her head his way, her face so pale he felt more murderous than ever.

"Michaels."

The gray-haired man lifted his head when Dane spoke his name. He frowned and straightened. "Who's he?" he barked, closing his hand around Hadley's arm. He was no taller than Hadley.

In the front hall, Dane could see the sheriff, armed, silently entering behind the man.

"It's okay, Alan," Hadley murmured. Her gaze clung to Dane's face. "It's just one of my boarders."

The man seemed to relax a little, the panic fading in his lined face. "That's right. You started a business for yourself. You were always so smart, Hannah. So smart." He looked at Hadley and tenderly touched her face. "I tried so hard to be what you wanted. Needed. Everything I ever did was for you." His voice dropped to a whisper. "Everything. You understand that, don't you?"

A tear slid down Hadley's face. "I understand, Alan."

The man nodded. Clearly relieved. He knelt down again and continued moving the broken mug away from Hadley's feet. "I don't want you to cut yourself," he said.

Shane stepped behind Michaels and planted his boot behind his back and the man went flat down on the floor, a squawk escaping him. "Don't move."

Dane swept Hadley into his arms, turning her away from the sight, holding her tightly. She was shaking like a leaf, and he pressed her head to his shoulder, shielding. On the floor Michaels was scrambling wildly against the sheriff, but he was outsized by Shane.

And when Michaels saw the gun in Shane's hand, he stopped struggling. He gave Hadley a beseeching look that Dane was glad she missed, then Michaels laid his head in the spill of coffee and started weeping. The shards of crockery he'd picked up fell from his bleeding hands.

Shane cuffed the man, his gaze cutting upward to his sister. "Hadley." His voice was sharp. Tight. "You all right?"

"He thinks I'm my mother," she whispered.

Dane looked down at the man, lying there, weeping softly. And he felt the knot of hatred he'd carried inside him for so long finally start to loosen.

Michaels was nothing but a sad ruin.

Shane hauled the man to his feet and pushed him down the hall to the door where Mandy had just arrived. She blew out a soundless whistle and followed the sheriff out. Dane knew his investigator would follow Michaels through his processing from start to finish and report back.

As long as Dane never had to see the man again, he'd be happy.

"Hannah," Michaels kept crying, even as the door closed behind them. "I love you. I've always loved you."

Hadley covered her mouth with her hand, her legs crumpling. Dane caught her up in his arms and carried her to her room. But as soon as he settled her on the bed, she scrambled off it and ran into the bathroom, slamming the door shut behind her.

He heard the sound of her retching. He went in.

She lifted her hand, staving him off, crying. "Don't."

He'd already let her send him away once.

He knelt down and carefully drew her long hair away from her face and she was sick again. He yanked a washcloth from the towel bar, dampened it and handed it to her.

She pressed it to her face, curling over on the fluffy yellow rug that covered much of the old-fashioned white tiles.

He leaned his head against the doorjamb and smoothed his hand slowly up and down her hunched back.

At least she could cry.

Chapter Thirteen

"Hadley?" Evie rushed into the kitchen, her children on her heels. "I just heard."

Her wide eyes skidded from Hadley to Dane where he leaned against the counter, then went back to Hadley once more. "Are you all right?" She dumped her coat and purse haphazardly on the counter and went over to her sister, pulling her into a tight hug.

Hadley nodded, looking over Evie's shoulder at Dane.

It had been less than an hour since Shane had hauled off Alan Michaels. She just couldn't bring herself to call that man her father. Beau Golightly was her father. And no other.

Dane's gaze was impenetrable and she looked away, pushing Evie aside and hugging her niece and nephews in one fell swoop.

Evie sort of collapsed into one of the other chairs. "Dad's on his way, too."

Hadley nodded. "He called." She smiled into Julie's face and tweaked Trevor's nose. "I really don't need everyone fussing. I'm...fine."

"Alan," Evie said. "Take Trev and Julie outside. You can play in the back by the windows here."

He nodded and ushered his siblings out the back door. Hadley bit her lip. "He seems so grown-up suddenly."

"I told them this morning that Charlie and I are getting a divorce," Evie said quietly.

Hadley's heart squeezed. "Oh, Evie." She reached across the table and grabbed her sister's hands. "I'm so sorry."

Evie shrugged. Her smile was sad. "I can't live with his affairs anymore, Had. Don't be sorry. This is a good decision for me. I'm just...gonna have to figure out what the heck I'm going to do to keep a roof over our heads."

"You'll come here," Hadley said immediately. "Of course you'll come here. Heavens, you should be running this place, and we both know it."

"Tiff's was your mom's place, Had."

"My mother and your father were married for nearly twenty years, Evie. She spent more time being your mother than anyone else did. Why *shouldn't* you run it?"

She sat forward, wondering why it took something like this to make her see the obvious. "It's the perfect ticket for you. We own the place free and clear. You can open up the extra rooms in the basement for the kids. You could keep the books just exactly the way you know they need to be. You're *always* telling me how I should be doing things here. So, just start doing them yourself!"

"But what about you?"

Hadley's vision blurred. She was painfully aware of Dane standing near the sink. "Tiff's was never my dream, Evie," she finally admitted the truth aloud. Knew that Dane was the only other one who'd seen it. "I took it over because it's what everyone else wanted me to do."

"And writing is your dream?"

Hadley nodded. For a very brief time she'd let herself think that Wood...*Dane*...might have a part in that dream. But that had been the biggest dream of all. A dream going in. A nightmare coming out.

"That's not going to pay your bills, either, Hadley," Evie said gently. "Not yet, anyway."

Hadley appreciated that last bit. "Then Stu can start paying me, and Riva can finally retire. And maybe I'll rent a room right here at Tiff's from my sister to save money while I'm at it."

Beau barreled into the room. "Honey?"

She'd begun thinking she might be able to hold it together. But the sight of her father undid that notion. She rose and went into his arms, hugging him tightly.

"Oh, Dad he was so...so sad."

"Shh." He kissed her forehead. Tilted her head back to look into her face. "It's over. Shane tells me Mr. Rutherford, there, has already arranged for Alan to be transferred to another institution. One not likely to be lax enough to lose him."

Hadley's gaze slid once more to Dane. Took in the total picture of him. Another expensive black sweater that draped his body to perfection and jeans that had never been sold in a small-town five-and-dime. "I guess when a Rutherford wants something done, it gets done," she said tightly.

Dane's eyes narrowed. His jaw flexed and he carefully turned to the sink. Poured the rest of his coffee down the drain and set aside the mug.

Then he walked out of the room.

"Hadley," Beau chided softly. "What was that about?"

But she could only shake her head. She pulled out of her dad's embrace and followed Dane.

He was heading toward the front door, his leather jacket gripped in his hand.

"So, you're leaving, then."

He stopped. Tilted back his head for a moment, a man seeking strength from some other source. "*My* father is still in a hospital bed," he reminded her after moment.

"Right." How she'd managed to push that detail to the side, she couldn't fathom.

She twisted her hands together. Took a halting step toward him. "Dane...oh, it feels so odd calling you that. And yet it fits you, so much better than Wood ever did." She was babbling. "I don't know what to say to you. I don't know what to do now."

"You don't have to do or say anything, Hadley. This was my doing. I warned you that I'd hurt you. It's the innocents who are always hurt." His expression was smooth, but the glimpse of his raw eyes—

that same glimpse she'd seen when he'd walked out of the kitchen—told her more than his words ever could. "But Michaels won't get to you again. I promise you that." He yanked open the door and went out.

Hadley caught the door before it closed behind him and stepped outside on the step. "And what about you, Dane?" she called after him as he headed down the steps. "Does it occur to you that you were one of those innocents yourself once? That Alan got to you more than he got to *any* of us?

"You told me yourself that your sister is a strong person. A healthy person. That she's married with children and living her own life. So what about you?"

He looked up at her, muttering a muffled curse. He took the steps again and yanked his coat around her shoulders. "You're gonna freeze yourself to death."

Her fingers caught his arms. *"What about you, Dane?"*

He glared at her. "I was sixteen and more interested in trying to score a date with a pretty girl in the elevator than keeping an eye on my kid sister. If I'd been doing what I was *supposed* to be doing, Michaels would never have had a chance to get his hands on Darby. But he did. And he kept her for four days, bound and gagged on a warehouse rooftop. Instead of blaming the one responsible, my parents blamed each other. And it was years before the legal dust of that particular war settled. There was *nothing* innocent about me."

"And if Michaels hadn't succeeded that day, do you think he wouldn't have tried another time? My mother left him before he could learn she was pregnant with me, and I was *six* when he tried that heinous stunt to win her back. He was desperate, Dane. Unbalanced. *That's* why he kidnapped your sister. So he could rescue her and be a hero in the eyes of a world that adored adoring the famous Rutherford kids. As if my mother would suddenly reappear in his life after spending so much careful effort to never be found by him. And after what happened here this morning it's clear he's *still* obsessed."

She shook her head. "I'm sorry, Dane. But you're blaming the wrong person in this. You've been holding on to your hatred for Alan Michaels all these years. But *you're* the one you won't forgive. You know, from the first day I met you I could see a kindness in you. Underneath the controlling exterior was a man who, who *felt.* I still believe that, Dane. No matter what your reasons were for using me, for—"

"I didn't use you!" His voice roared over her. "I loved you. I took one look at your face through the cracked windshield of my friend's car and knew I'd never be the same. You think that was *using* you? I came to this godforsaken town because of Michaels. Period."

Hadley's lips parted. "And I'm his…daughter."

"You're Holly and Beau Golightly's daughter," he snapped. "Michaels just unknowingly contributed some sperm along the way. And I didn't know any of that when I took you into my bed! Or when you saw me for the liar I was and told me to leave.''

"I thought you knew.''

"I didn't. So I guess that's one thing I *haven't* lied about.'' He stomped down the steps.

"Two,'' she called after him.

His boots stopped. "Two what?''

"Two things you haven't lied about.'' She descended the steps and caught up to him. Slid the coat off her shoulders and deftly pulled it around him, instead. "You're gonna freeze yourself to death,'' she repeated his words back to him.

He grabbed her wrists, holding her hands away from him as if he couldn't bear her touch. His jacket slid off his wide shoulders and crumpled on the cold sidewalk at their feet. "What *two* things?'' His voice was clipped.

"That you love me.''

His jaw flexed. "Well, believe me, sweetness. I don't expect you to return the favor.''

"Love is never a favor. It's a gift.''

"Spoken like a woman who believes in forgiveness.'' He let go of her wrists. "Go back inside, Hadley, where you belong.''

"Because I could never belong in *your* world?''

"Because I could never belong in *yours*.'' His voice was raw. "Life doesn't exist for me like it does for you, Hadley. I don't have choices. I have my father's legacy. Rutherford Industries. And it doesn't go away just because I wish it would.''

"Oh, Dane.'' Her eyes burned. "You're doing the same thing I've been doing all my life. Filling expectations for someone else at the expense of your own dreams.''

"Maybe so," he allowed. "But there's not one damn thing I can do about it." His lips twisted. "I'm a Rutherford. I'm not devaluing you, Hadley. But my playing field is a helluva lot different from yours."

"Yes. But being a Rutherford isn't the only thing that you are." She closed her arms around herself. "You're the only man I've ever loved."

Pain ripped over his face, not masked quickly enough for her to miss, and her heart broke open just that much more. "My mother and Beau were married for twenty years. If she hadn't died of cancer, they'd have still been going strong at twenty more."

She smiled but her eyes burned. "She told me once that by the second day after meeting Beau, she'd known she'd love him all the days of her life. And she did. Maybe I'm more like my mother than I ever dreamed."

"Hadley." Her name tore from his lips. "Don't."

"You can walk away from me, Dane. But that's not going to change what I feel. Or what you feel, if you really meant those words. It's just going to mean we're not sharing what we feel together. And frankly, well, frankly choosing to waste that particular gift *does* seem unforgivable. I love you. I will always love you. But maybe you have to stop hating yourself for something that someone else did before you can accept that."

His hands opened. Closed.

"Go to your father, Dane," she whispered.

"What are you going to do?"

She picked up his coat. Held it close for a moment. It smelled of him. But she knew she didn't need to keep the jacket near to remember everything there was to remember about him.

"You heard me in there. I'm going to talk Stu into giving me a paying job for once. And I'm going to stop writing in notebooks and start writing on a computer. I want to be a writer and I'm going to start acting like it instead of playing at it. I'm going to live my life, Dane." She pushed the jacket into his hand. "And I'm going to keep on loving you whether or not you figure out how to live your own life, too."

Then she turned and went back up the steps.

Dane exhaled. He stood there on the sidewalk, feeling the cold Montana wind cutting through his clothes.

The door to Tiff's remained closed.

Hadley did not come back out.

And it felt as if something vital inside him died.

"Are you out of your tree?" Roth Rutherford was sitting in his favorite chair in the office he kept at the expansive compound that had been Dane's home growing up. "What do you mean you're resigning as CEO? Do you want to give me another heart attack?"

"You're not likely to have one," Dane said pointedly, "since your surgery three months ago." He looked out the window. Miles of green Kentucky grass rolled over the gentle hills, cordoned off tidily by the planks of pristine white fencing. "And I'm not resigning. I *have* resigned. The PR department issued a statement a few hours ago. It'll be in the evening editions."

"I don't care what the papers print. You can't resign until the board votes on it. And I'm still a senior member of that board."

"Darby's already agreed to vote my way."

"Darby! She gives me her proxies."

"Not this time."

Roth glared at him. Together, Darby's and Dane's votes outnumbered Roth's by one. "And just what in Hades do you figure you're gonna *do?*"

Dane sat down and faced his father across the coffee table. "I'm going to build cars again," he said evenly. "Custom racing. RTM. It's my company just as much as Rutherford Industries was yours. And I've neglected it long enough."

"Never could get that racing bug outta you," Roth muttered. He pushed out of his chair. "Stubborn cuss."

"He comes by that rather honestly, now doesn't he?"

Dane looked over to the woman lounging near the window hung with yards of pale blue silk. Even after all these months he wasn't used to the sight of his mother being a regular presence in the house again.

"Nobody asked for your opinion, Felicia."

"You're getting it anyway, Roth." She merely turned another page of the magazine she was reading. "He's my son, too."

"Don't you have some shopping or something to do?"

Dane shoved his hands through his hair. "You two

deserve each other,'' he muttered. But there was still satisfaction in knowing his parents had come to some sort of peace accord since Roth's surgery.

''So you're bound and determined on going to Indy?'' Roth's voice was still cantankerous.

''I'm not—'' He broke off when Marlene entered the room.

She set a tray of crustless sandwiches on the table near Roth. ''Sims called up from the security gate,'' she said. ''There's someone here to see you, Dane.''

''Probably Fitzpatrick wanting a statement on the press release,'' Dane said. ''I've already told him when I do give a statement, he'll have an exclusive. He can just sit on his thumbs until I'm good and ready.'' The reporter had been covering his family for years. Had spent many hours camped outside the compound waiting for whatever tidbit the public could waste their time on when it came to ''The'' Rutherfords.

''It's not Fitzpatrick. Though he's probably out there getting plenty of close-ups. Sims said it was a woman. Golightly?'' Marlene shook her head. ''Probably just another stunt, with a name like that, but—''

Dane strode past her through the house that was filled with more antiques than some museums. His boots rang out on the marble floor, echoing slightly in the foyer before he pushed out the wide front entrance. His car was parked in the circular drive and he slid behind the wheel gunning it down the wide, curved road past the stone fountains and statuary garden before reaching the security gate.

As soon as he neared it, the massive iron swung open and he slowed. Stopped.

A plain white rental car was parked next to the guard's booth. Hadley stood on the narrow strip of concrete next to it. Her long dark hair drifted in the afternoon breeze.

And even though it was nearly May, she wore a soft pink jacket with her narrow blue jeans.

Then she turned, and looked at him across the yards still separating them. Her hands twisted together at her waist.

She was the most beautiful sight he'd ever seen.

He climbed from the car and shut the door. He slowly closed the short distance between them.

Her eyes were wide. The darkest brown. And they searched his face when he stopped in front of her.

"Hi."

"Hi." Her voice was soft. "You—" She pressed her lips together for a moment. "Your forehead looks a lot better."

"Not too scarred up?"

A lock of hair danced across her face, caught by the whispering breeze. "Never."

"See you got the jacket."

She blinked and looked down at herself, her fingers smoothing over the garment. "It came yesterday. You didn't have to, you know."

"I know." The jacket was somewhat different from the one she'd worn the day they'd crashed into each other's lives. For one thing, he was certain that her original one hadn't come from Milan.

But it was the same color and that's what he'd wanted.

"Is that what you came here for, Hadley? To thank me in person for the coat?"

She swallowed and took a step closer to him. "How's your father?"

"Ornery. Pissed as hell at me at the moment." He shoved his hands in his pockets. "In better health now than he has been for years."

"That's good. And, um, your sister?"

"She's fine. Her husband and kids are fine. My mother's fine. Have we covered everyone?"

She shook her head. "Not even close."

He looked across the road. Sure enough, Fitzpatrick was sitting in his van, a long telephoto lens visible through the window.

"Come on." He reached out and tucked his hand around her elbow and tried hard to ignore the jolt that touching her had always caused as he drew her back through the gate. It immediately slid shut behind her. "You're probably going to find your photograph on the news wires tonight."

Her eyebrows rose. "What are you talking about?"

"That's a reporter sitting in the van over there."

"Good heavens." Her gaze skipped from the van to his vintage roadster to the expansive grounds. "I don't think we're in Kansas anymore," she murmured. "Do I…is it okay to leave my car out there? I rented it at the airport."

"It's fine." He opened the passenger door, and she slid into the low seat. He rounded the car and got in behind the wheel and drove out of sight of the gate. But he stopped before they reached the house.

She was eyeing the mammoth structure ahead of them, her jaw slightly dropped. "Oh, my."

"It's just a house."

Her gaze slanted his way. "Just?" She shook her head a little, but her lips twitched. "That's like saying Niagara Falls is just a water spill."

"What are you really here for, Hadley?"

Her faint smile died. Her lashes dipped. "I missed you," she said baldly. "And I thought…well, when the jacket arrived—" She shook her head. "I'd hoped—"

"Hoped what?"

"That it meant you had forgiven me," she said on a rush and pushed out of the car.

He got out more slowly and followed her over to the lush grass that lined the drive. "Forgive *you*. For what?" Being the light he saw whenever he shut his eyes?

"For…everything. What I said to you. I'm the daughter of Alan Michaels."

His lips tightened. "Are we going to dwell on that for the rest of our lives, Hadley? *I* had more exposure to the guy than you ever did. He's in a private sanitarium in Canada now."

"Private?" She looked startled. "But how?"

"Money. If you've got enough of it, you can make just about anything happen. Michaels is fine. You don't have to worry about him. He's not living out his days in shackles and chains. He's got nearly every comfort of home without the freedom of ever being a danger to you or anyone else.''

She searched his face. ''You're paying for it, aren't you?'' she asked slowly. ''But why? You, your family, of all people you owe him nothing.''

''Following his fascination with Lucius led me to you.''

Her lips parted soundlessly. Her eyes suddenly glistened. ''Dane.''

''The jacket is just a gift, Hadley. No strings attached.''

''Oh.'' She didn't quite look at him. ''I see.''

He exhaled roughly and reached for her. ''Do you? I've resigned as CEO, sweetness. Rutherford Industries and I are parting ways. The news'll hit the financials by tomorrow.''

Her gaze flew to his. Wide. Searching. ''Why?''

He pulled her closer. Where he could inhale the soft fragrance of her silky hair. ''To live my life. Isn't that what you said I needed to learn how to do?''

''And have you?'' Her voice was husky.

He touched her hair. Slowly drew it back from her lovely face. ''I'm beginning to.''

''Oh, Dane.''

He'd never tire of hearing his name on her lips. ''I have another gift for you.'' His voice was low.

''What?''

''My love.''

She inhaled sharply.

He gently caught her head between his hands, his gaze boring into hers. ''But I'm not kind like you.

My gift comes with strings. A lot of them. A lifetime of them. Did you come here only to say thanks for the coat?''

She shook her head. A tear slipped down her cheek. ''I came here because I was afraid you wouldn't come to me. Not after I said those unforgivable things to you that day.''

''Not unforgivable, sweetness.'' He softly kissed her lips. ''Only true. Of all the people in my life, Hadley, you were the only one to ever see the truth.''

Her lids had gone heavy. She swayed against him, her fingers kneading his shoulders. He wanted to lift her against him and find the nearest bed. He brushed his thumb across her lips.

She closed her eyes for a moment, shuddering a little. ''What are the strings?''

Had anything ever mattered more than this moment? This woman? She'd lit every corner inside him. ''Marriage. To me.''

Her lashes lifted, and the tears in her eyes slowly began slipping past her lashes. ''Dane. Are you sure?''

''Nothing less will do. I warned you, sweetness. *Strings.*''

She touched his face. Gently drew her hand down his cheek. ''I'm just a girl from Lucius. And you're—''

''The only man you've ever loved,'' he finished. ''Unless you've changed your mind.''

She shook her head. ''I haven't changed my mind. Or my heart. I love you.'' She twined her arms around his neck, pulling his head down to hers.

And he felt the smile growing on her lips as she pressed her mouth to his.

"Yes, Dane Rutherford," she answered, her voice soft. Sure. "Bring on those strings."

Epilogue

The center aisle of the Lucius Community Church had never looked so long.

Hadley stood in the vestibule, listening to the sound of the strings filling the small church with their beautiful strains.

Shane leaned down. "Don't think I've ever heard that many violins in one small church before."

Hadley smiled a little. "Dane's idea." His brand of humor. Strings everywhere. In the four weeks since she'd gone to Dane, he'd proven over and over just how serious he'd been in that score.

Evie tugged gently on Hadley's floor-length veil, making sure it hung just so over the chapel-length train of Hadley's embroidered silk gown. "You're sure you want to do this?" she asked in a voice low enough that Darby—also a bridesmaid—couldn't hear. "Even if he is a Rutherford, if you're not sure, you can always change your mind. Just because this was the fastest wedding on record ever planned, doesn't mean—"

"Don't worry so, Evie."

Darby slid an amused glance her way. She lowered her eyelid in a barely noticeable wink. Like Evie, she wore a slender dress of palest green. With the church adorned with ivy and orange blossoms in every pew and pillar, the two women were like lovely flowers in a garden.

Evie breathed out a long breath. "Okay, then." She looked around for Julie. "Come on, sweetheart. It's almost time."

Hadley's niece stopped preening at her reflection in the windows surrounding the door and joined her mother. "You look pretty, Auntie Hadley."

"So do you, Julie." Julie's dress was also green with yards of lace. She looked like a princess.

Alan just rolled his eyes. But he made certain that the rings tied to his satin pillow were safely in place and that the tie at his neck was still straight.

The violins swelled and on cue, Dane's sister stepped forward. Evie sent Hadley another quick smile, then she nudged Alan and Julie through the door. A moment later she followed them.

Heading up the aisle.

That long, *long* aisle.

An unaccountable panic settled in Hadley's chest. Her hand tightened around Shane's arm.

The church was packed to the gills with guests.

Dane's parents were in the front row on the groom's side. Joanie and Mrs. Ardelle and Vince were sitting on her side. There was a collection of vans parked outside the church, waiting to get a shot of the American prince and the small-town girl who'd won his heart.

What if she tripped on the deep-red runner that lined the aisle?

What if she fell on her face when they left the church after the ceremony?

What if she was making the biggest mistake of her life?

Shane covered her fingers with his hand and squeezed gently. "You okay, turnip?"

The strings shifted melodies to the bridal march. Darby, Evie and the children had reached the front of the church where Beau stood, resplendent in his black robes, his well-worn bible held in his hand. On the other side of him, the groomsmen were lined up, looking handsome in their black suits. The *real* Wood Tolliver. Stu. Young Trevor.

"Had?"

She barely heard her brother.

Dane had moved into place, and his gaze found hers.

The aisle suddenly didn't seem any longer than it ever had before.

He was waiting for her. This man whose life had collided with hers. This man who loved her. Totally.

Completely.

And all of her silly little fears slid away.

"Do you believe in fate, Shane?"

He frowned a little and she smiled, taking pity on him. Her brother had never been one for talking about matters of the heart. She lifted her bouquet of white orchids a little higher in front of her exquisite white gown. Dane had brought in a designer to prepare it in a sinfully short period of time.

Fate. Destiny. Miracles. It didn't matter what word she used. God had brought Dane into her life and there he would stay.

She exhaled, her gaze focused only on him. She had the strongest sense that her mother was with her and that Holly approved. "I'm fine, Shane. In fact, everything is absolutely perfect."

There was nothing to fear. Not ever again. Whatever life brought them, she and Dane would be together.

Then she stepped forward, surely and without hesitation, to embrace their future.

* * * * *

*Be sure to watch for
Nikki's romance, coming only to
Silhouette Special Edition in 2005.*

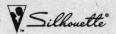

SPECIAL EDITION™

This January 2005...don't miss
the next book in bestselling author

Victoria Pade's

brand-new miniseries...

Northbridge Nuptials

Where a walk down the aisle is never far behind.

HAVING THE BACHELOR'S BABY

(SE #1658)

After sharing one incredible night in the arms of
Ben Walker, Clair Cabot is convinced she'll never
see the sexy reformed bad boy again. Then fate
throws her for a loop when she's forced to deal
with Ben in a professional capacity. Should she
also confess the very personal secret that's
growing in her belly?

Available at your favorite retail outlet.

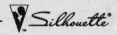

SPECIAL EDITION™

Be there for every emotional moment
of the new miniseries

BAYSIDE BACHELORS

and discover why readers love Judy Duarte!

From bad boys to heroes…
through the love of a good woman

She didn't believe in heroes; Hailey Conway believed in
making a good, predictable life for herself. Until San Diego
detective Nick Granger saved her from a mugger and
swept her off her feet—and into his bed. Now, with a baby
on the way and Nick haunting her dreams, Hailey knew
the rugged rebel might break her heart…or become
the hero who saved it.

HAILEY'S HERO
by Judy Duarte

Silhouette Special Edition #1659
On sale January 2005!

Meet more Bayside Bachelors later this year!

THEIR SECRET SON—Available February 2005
WORTH FIGHTING FOR—Available May 2005
THE MATCHMAKER'S DADDY—Available June 2005

Only from Silhouette Books!

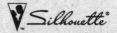

eHARLEQUIN.com

The Ultimate Destination for Women's Fiction

For **FREE online reading,** visit
www.eHarlequin.com now and enjoy:

Online Reads
Read **Daily** and **Weekly** chapters from
our Internet-exclusive stories by your
favorite authors.

Interactive Novels
Cast your vote to help decide how these
stories unfold...then stay tuned!

Quick Reads
For shorter romantic reads, try our
collection of Poems, Toasts, & More!

Online Read Library
Miss one of our online reads?
Come here to catch up!

Reading Groups
Discuss, share and rave with other
community members!

For great reading online,
visit www.eHarlequin.com today!

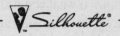

SPECIAL EDITION™

Don't miss the latest heartwarming tale from new author

Mary J. Forbes!

Ex-cop Jon Tucker was doing just fine living by his lonesome. Until his alluring new neighbor moved in next door, reminding him of everything he thought he'd left behind—family, togetherness, love. In fact, single mother Rianne Worth had awakened a yearning inside him so sweet he was hard-pressed to resist…especially when giving in to her meant becoming a family man, again.

A FATHER, AGAIN

Silhouette Special Edition #1661
On sale January 2005!

Only from Silhouette Books!